THROUGH

THE

STORM

I0519918

Written By

Dion Williams

"MY PAIN"

I've been hurt.

But most of you don't understand.

The WOUNDS, and BRUISES That conceal My Body.

It's like I'm living on a HORRIBLE Land.

The Things that I see. The things that he does to me.

I just wanna break away, and be FREE.

I'm here Hostage in my own SOUL.

Wrapped up by CHAINS that I can't let GO.

I Try and hide, but it seems like he just comes from the other side. In My mind I cry NO,

But My Body is telling me to GROW.

I know what I want to be, but the Pain keeps

FIGHTING Me. My BLOOD screams as it's getting EXPOSED,

But this ain't the way my Life 'supposed to go.

No matter what anybody says to me.

I'm gonna Break away and be THE BEAUTIFUL ME

-Dionnica Elizabeth Williams

Here is a person with great ambition that wants to make it on her own in the world. As she goes out to pursue this dream, she goes through trials and ordeals that one may wonder whether she can survive in the madness of the world. Her strength and faith in higher power led and guided her "Through the storm"…

CHAPTER ONE

"SO IT BEGINS"

"Man, it sure is hot out here today," Pam said to herself as she waited on the bus to go home from another day at work. "Where is this bus today? Dang!" As she stared to sweat, the bus finally arrived and she got on.

"Hey Pam," the bus driver said to her.

She said, "Hi John."

"Sorry, but I was caught in traffic," John said as Pam took her seat.

"That's okay," Pam said. "I'm just glad you got here. I thought that I was going to melt out there." John had been taking her to her job for three years now, so they were on first name basis. As they pulled up to her home, John told her, "Same time in the morning and don't you be late, okay?"

As Pam got off, she said, "I will see you in the morning. Bye."

See, John would wait on her in the morning when she was running behind, even if he had people on the bus. As he pulled off, she entered her home, well, her parents' home, and she said hello to everyone: her mom, dad, brother, and sister. They all greeted her, but Pam was so tired she went to her room and lay across her bed.

Her dad came in and said, "Baby, you okay?"

She replied, "Yes, just a little tired, but I only need 20 minutes to wind down."

Her dad said, "Okay baby, your food is in the microwave waiting on you when you are ready for it," and kissed her on the forehead as he walked out of the room.

"Thanks, Dad," Pam said.

Dad said, "You are always welcome, sweetheart."

Pam was 18 years old, and she had her mind made up that when she got out of high school, she was going to get her own place, because she knew that was what she wanted to do. Pam felt like college wasn't for her, and that she could make it in the world with the knowledge and wisdom she had from growing up and knowing the Lord. She felt like since she was the oldest out of the kids, she wanted them to look up to her like they looked up to her daddy. She was not trying to out-do him, but she loved what her daddy had taught her about life.

After 20 minutes went by, Pam got up and went into the room where everybody was, saying, "I'm sorry. I just needed to get my head back a little bit."

The whole family was like, "Don't worry. We are glad to just see you."

As Pam got her food, her brother came up to her, kissed her on her cheek, and said, "I'm so glad to be your brother, because you got some fine friends. HA! HA! HA!"

As Pam bowed him in the chest, she said, "Boy, shut up."

Her brother was the high school player, not in sports, but with the women, and his sister knew a lot of girls, because she was also well-known. However, she wasn't wild at all, but was really pretty. "Man, sit down with your nasty self," said Pam.

Her brother replied with his hands up and a sneaky grin on his face. "Man, what did I do?"

"Anyway . . ." Pam said as she sat down to eat. " . . . OOOH! Who cooked this chicken?" She knew both of her parents could cook.

"Your daddy, honey," her mother said. "You know how he is with his chicken. Won't tell nobody what he puts in it, and hell, I taught him how to cook. Now he is trying . . . well damn, he is out-cooking me!"

"Baby, I just want you to enjoy life and sit back while your man cooks for you," her dad said while kissing and hugging her mom.

"Ya'll so crazy," said Pam. When she finished, she told her parents that she needed to talk to them later on about something. They looked concerned and asked if everything was all right. She said with a smile, "Yes, ya'll, it's all good. We just need to talk." Then she proceeded back to her room.

As the night got later, her parents came to her door and knocked to see if she was still up. Pam said, "Come in, I'm just lying here." They went in and asked her what was wrong. Pam sat up in the bed and replied, "Nothing is wrong with me, I'm fine."

Her dad said, "Well, what do you need to talk to us about?"

"Nothing really, I'm just . . . well . . . I don't know." Pam folded her arms in confusion. "I just feel like I need to get my own place, you know? Live on my own now. I know I'm not going to college. I really love the job I'm at right now." She looked at both of them with a look of sorrow, but happiness was in her eyes. "Daddy, you got me a job that only college people can get and I've been there for three years. You and Mom have showed me how to budget and pay bills by letting me help ya'll out when ya'll needed it."

Then Mom said, "Well, that's true, baby, but you are only 18. Don't you think you're moving a little too fast?"

"No," said Pam. "When will I be ready, then? When I'm stuck and don't have a clue what I want to do in life; then what?"

Her parents put their heads down and her dad said, "Baby girl, it's your call. We will back you 100%, whatever it may be."

Pam got out of the bed, hugged them both, and said, "I love ya'll so much."

As she went back to bed and her parents were going out the door, her dad turned around and said, "You don't have somebody, do you? Some man trying to make you move?"

Pam said "No! It's just me, myself, and I. Okay, Daddy?"

"Okay, pumpkin, just checking."

Her mom pulled him out of the room, saying, "Bring your butt on and leave that child alone."

The next morning, like clockwork, she was on the bus. "Good morning," she said to John.

He replied, "Good morning to you as well. What are you so happy about at this time of morning? You haven't been this happy since the last day of school. Ha! Ha! Ha!"

"Well, since you must know, I'm thinking about getting my own place and being my own woman." She was smiling ear to ear as she told John the good news.

He just smiled and said, "Do what you feel you got to do and I'm proud of you for already knowing what you are going to do in life."

John had kids as well, but a little different than Pam. His daughter was pregnant at 15 and now she was 21, still staying at home, and his son that was 26 years old just moved back home with two kids of his own from a marriage that went sour. So he was happy to see that Pam was on the right track and knew what she wanted.

As they pulled up to her job, she saw her daddy leaving. She waved at him as he shouted out that he loved her. She shouted back, "I love you, too!"

Her dad worked the graveyard shift while Pam worked in the morning in the office. Her dad had been there so long he used to bring his daughter to work with him when she was little, so she pretty much knew everyone there before she got hired. He had been there more than 30 years.

He'd offered to buy Pam a car, but Pam didn't want a car; she just asked her dad to give her the money and she put it in the bank. Pam was a very independent woman that had set her goals early in life. She had been just focusing on life, not its downfalls. She had no boyfriend because she saw her friends get pregnant early. She went out to events, but not that many where everybody knew who she was. She was just a girl who'd seen her parents do well, and she just wanted the same. It was Friday, and the day ended. She got home and as the family said hello, she said, "It's Friday and it's the weekend. Yes!" She and Dad didn't have to work on the weekends, so they just did family things, but her brother, a typical male, was going out with the fellas to a game, so they just chilled, played Uno, and watched movies.

Pam said, "Well, it's about 10, so I think I will turn in." The family asked why so soon, and she said, "Because I got to get up in the morning along with Daddy to look for a place."

Her dad looked surprised and said, "You are really serious, aren't you?"

Pam said, "Yes, and we can play and watch movies over at my place." She turned with a cool stroll down the hall saying, "Dad, I will see you in the morning. I love ya'll."

As morning broke, Pam could barely sleep. She was so excited about going to look for her own place that she was already dressed and ready to go before her father could make it into the room. Good. "Wow," her father said, "I see you are already ready to leave us."

"Now Daddy, stop that nonsense." Pam said.

"Why are you talking to me like that?" her father responded.

"Like what, Father?" Pam said.

"Like that!" Daddy replied. "All the 'Father' crap. What is really going on with you, Pam? You're acting a little too loose for me and I don't like that."

"Dad," she said as she tried to hug him with anger on his face, "I'm just happy."

"Well, don't be doing me like that. I don't like that," he said. "I just want to know the real reason you're trying to get out of here so quick. Tell me something. Hell, I deserve to know that much, don't I?"

"Yes, you do," Pam said, "and there's nothing going on with me but life." She was still hugging her daddy tightly. "I promise you that everything is fine."

"So where are you going to look for this place?" Daddy asked.

She said, "I really don't know, but I would like for it to be somewhere close to here and my job." They went out together to find a place for her. As they were looking, nothing really caught her eye, but all of a sudden, Pam cried out, "Look at those! Turn in there."

Dad turned in the apartments that were gated and had a guard at the gate. As they drove up, the guard asked, "Can I help you?"

Her dad said, "Yes, my daughter is looking for an apartment." The guard asked for their I.D.s, and made them sign a form before they could enter. After they were finished, he told them how to get to the leasing center, and then let the gate open.

While in route to the office, Pam said, "I feel safe already." She laughed with her dad as they pulled up to the office. When they walked in, the people were very polite to her and her father. They just told them that they had a one bedroom all ready to go if they would like to see it. Pam said, "Yes, let's go." When they got on the apartment's golf cart to go see the unit, Pam was full of excitement and her legs were shaking.

"Baby, come down here," Dad said. "You haven't even seen the place yet and already you're going crazy." They pulled up to the apartment and entered, and it was very nice. The leasing agent showed them around and told them it already came with an alarm system, cable, and washer and dryer.

The lady told them the price, and Pam said, "Wow, that's kind of high, but once you factor in everything, that's fair, I guess." So, they went back up front and talked about the apartment. It just so happened that the head owner of the apartments was in the office. The lady told them who he was and introduced them to him.

The owner said, "So, are ya'll renting an apartment?"

"Well, I'm not, but my daughter is, but it is a little too much for her to keep it up."

So the owner said, "Well, how much you plan on spending a month for an apartment?"

Pam said, "At least $200 cheaper than that."

The owner said. "Wow! Well, I'm sure that you will find something like that and you already filled out everything. Here is my card if you change your mind."

Pam took the card and said, "Thank you." They left, and Pam told her dad, "Let's just go home. We have been out all day. I'm tired." They went home and she was looking out the window, seeing that everything from stores, restaurants, and her bus was all right there. She was thinking that everything she needed was right there for her.

When they got home, her mom asked, "Did ya'll have any luck today?"

Pam said, "No, there was this one place, but it was a little too much for me."

Her mom said, "Well, baby, you just wait. Something will come for you."

"Yeah, I guess so," Pam replied, and went to her room to take off her clothes and put on something relaxing. As the night came to an end, Pam went to sleep. She was so tired that the next morning, she jumped up and said, "Oh my God, I'm late for work."

She rushed and took a shower, put on her clothes, and darted toward the front door when her brother said, "Girl, where are you going in a rush?"

She said, "To work. I'm late."

Her brother said, "You have to work on Sunday now?"

"Sunday?" Pam replied.

"Yes, it is Sunday. You need to calm down. You are trying to do too much."

"Man, you are right," Pam said to her brother as she flopped down on the sofa and put her purse to the side of her. She put her head in her hands and took a deep breath. "Okay, let me get my head back in order." As she was talking to herself, everybody got up to see what was going on.

Her brother said, "Pam thought it was Monday, so she was heading out the door to go to work."

"Baby, what is going on?" her mother asked her as she sat next to her on the sofa and put her arm around her.

"Nothing, I just need to get my head back in order," Pam said.

"Don't let this moving thing stress you out like this. It's not that serious," her dad said to her. "So just take a moment and put yourself back together, okay?"

"You're right, Dad. I will take a moment and get myself back together," said Pam, "and I know just how to do it. I'm going to church early, since I'm already dressed and everything."

"Well, we all can go since we're up," said her mother.

"Come on, ya'll. Can't we just go back to sleep," said her brother.

"No!" both of their parents shouted. "Now, go get dressed."

As Pam's brother walked past her, he mumbled to her, "I should've said nothing and let your butt go to work."

CHAPTER TWO

"GOING INTO THE WORLD"

They arrived at church and they all had a great time. They really connected with the message. As they were leaving, Pam and her dad saw the owner of the apartments that Pam liked so much. "Is that the man from the apartments, Dad?" Pam asked.

"Yes, it is him. I didn't know he went to this church," her daddy said.

"Me either," Pam replied.

As they approached him, he looked up and said, "Hey, what a small world, huh?" He hugged Pam and shook her dad's hand. "So, ya'll visiting or something?" he asked.

"No, we are members here. We've been here for years," her dad said, "and this is the rest of the family." He introduced the entire family to him.

"Wow! I have been here a while myself and I also work on the board here in the church."

"Wow!" Pam said. "But we always come to the second service. We just came this morning because I thought it was Monday, so I just stayed up and here we are," she said with an embarrassing look on her face smile.

"Well, that's okay. As long as you made it here, that's enough," the owner said. "Well, let me not hold ya'll up, and be blessed. Right Pam?"

"Yes," Pam replied.

"You have my number. Just give me a call when you are ready," the owner said.

"I will," Pam said. "Thank you and good seeing you again." They both said their goodbyes and went their separate ways.

As they were riding in the car, the dad said, "Let's go out to dinner as a family, because I don't want to cook today. It's too hot to be standing in a kitchen." They all agreed, went to a nice restaurant, ate, and came home. They stayed up a little bit, and went to bed.

As they were going to bed, Pam's brother said, "Now, for real, you have to go to work tomorrow," and started laughing.

"Boy, anyway, shut up," Pam said to her brother, "and goodnight."

The morning came and her day at work went pretty fast. As she was sitting on the bus, her phone rang. "Hello," Pam said.

"May I speak to Pam Williams, please?"

"This is she. Who's calling?" she asked.

"This is Mrs. Johnson from Eagle Land Apartments." As she heard that name, she realized it was from the apartments that she liked. "How are you today, Ms. Williams?" the manager asked.

"I'm fine," Pam said.

"I was calling to tell you that, for some reason, the owner said to let you have the apartment for three hundred dollars less than what it is listed at, and it is locked in, regardless if we raise our rates. Your lease remains the same as long as you want it to be."

Pam screamed on the bus and everybody looked at her, trying to figure out what was going on. She said, "Yes, yes, I will take it," to the woman on the phone.

"Well, you let us know when you are ready to move in and we will handle the rest, okay?"

"I sure will, and thank you for everything." She hung up the phone. "Yes! I got it!" she said out loud on the bus.

John, the bus driver, said, "Got what?"

"The apartment, and you will still be picking me up, because it is still on your route, but you go past it before you pick me up."

"Oh, ok, that's great. Congratulations to you."

"Thanks," and she hugged John as she got off the bus and told everybody goodbye. She ran into the house, where everybody heard the good news about her apartment.

"That's great for you," her mother said.

And her brother said, "Oh yeah, now I have somewhere I can chill."

"Oh no, buddy, none of that at my house. You can just hang that thought up."

Her brother started laughing and saying, "I was just playing, sis. You fine." He put his arm around her shoulder and pulled her closer to him. "But seriously, let me come over sometimes with my friend to watch the house while you're gone. I can watch it so that nobody comes in when you're not there."

"We got security for that. Anyway, you would not be watching; you would be trying to do other things," said Pam. "I'm no fool. Now, get off of me." She moved his arm from around her shoulder.

"So, when are you supposed to move?" her dad asked.

"That part is up to me, so I really have to think about that for a minute," Pam said with a smiley face.

"Well, just take your time and let us know when so that we can help you with everything."

"Okay," Pam replied, as she got ready for dinner.

Her mother was so proud of her that she started to cry as she prepared food for the family. "Lord, thank you," she said while looking up in the sky from the kitchen. "Thank you, Jesus, for teaching me and my husband how to be good parents to our kids and thank you for not allowing trouble come our way when we are in a time of need. Thank you for allowing my daughter to be determined to make something out of herself in her young life, and protect her as she moves forward."

As Pam's mother was over in the kitchen, her father walked behind her and said, "We did pretty good with our kids, huh?"

"Yes, we did. Yes, we did," Pam's mom said as she grabbed his hand. "Well, let's sit down and eat now. Come on, baby girl, and help me set the table for dinner," her mother said to the youngest child.

She really looked up to Pam, and told her mom, "I'm sad, but happy."

"Why is that?" the mother asked.

"I don't know. I guess, well, is Pam ever going to come back and play with me or teach me things like she used to?"

"Yes, baby, she isn't going to leave you like that. She is just around the corner. You can go over her house sometimes and visit. I know she wouldn't mind that at all."

"Really cool, because she really has taught me a lot in my life, and I don't want her to stop being that way with me," Pam's sister said.

"She won't. She is just turning into a woman, and she is moving to another level in her life and, someday, you will be doing the same thing," Mom said to her daughter, "so, just be happy for her, and let her know that you are excited as well, okay?"

"Okay, Mommy, I will." They both sat at the table and ate dinner. The night was great, and everybody went to sleep.

Pam called the apartment people the next day when she was on break at work, and asked when was the quickest she could move into the apartment. The manager said, "When do you want to?"

"I don't know, this weekend, I guess," Pam replied.

"Okay, let me check and I will get back to you before the day is out."

"Okay, that's fine. Just leave me a message if I don't answer the phone," Pam said to the manager, since she was at work and didn't want anything to go wrong by her being on the phone, or to do anything that could get her in trouble. Even though she had never gotten in trouble and her daddy had been there a long time, she knew that it was still her job, and she didn't want to jeopardize that.

The manager said, "I sure will do that."

"Thank you," Pam said, and hung up the telephone.

As the day went by, Pam got so busy that when she got home, she was so tired that she forgot to see if anybody had called her. No one at home said anything, because she looked like she was really tired. It wasn't until the next morning while she was on the bus that she realized to check her phone and see if anybody had called her. Sure enough, she had two messages in her phone. One was from a girlfriend, and the other one was from the apartments, saying that one was ready, she could move in that weekend, and that they were waving the deposit for her, as well. Pam was so happy that she called the leasing office and left a message to thank them, knowing that no one was there at that time. She started working, but every now and then, they had a day at work where they stayed extra hours to catch up with everybody in the building. Also, inventory had to go out quarterly, and today was that day. She'd had a rough day before, but this was the kicker. As the day went on, she was once again tired, and really had no energy to do anything but get home and get ready to hit it again the next day at work. Before she could catch her breath, the whole week was a monster at work. After she found out about the inventory, she knew that those particular weeks would be long ones, and she really forgot about a lot of things; she just focused on what was going on at work. Nevertheless, Pam had been there three years. She just did what needed to be done and tried to grind it out the best she could.

Everyone at work was so tired from working so hard that they didn't realize Friday had arrived. The head boss came in and told them this was a job well done, and that he was proud of them and what they had done. He bought lunch for everybody in the office. Everyone in the office had a sigh of relief over their heads. As Pam started to slow down and get herself in order, she started hearing a buzzing sound. It was coming from her purse. She realized it was her phone, and she reached in and had 10 messages. It had been so tough at work that she didn't even check her phone. She'd worked so hard that she forgot about everything, even the apartment. At lunchtime, she checked her phone. Some messages were from her friends, and the others were from the apartment people letting her know the number of the apartment and that she could move in after 9:00 a.m.

She was amazed she could move in so soon. She called her dad, who was also tired. Her mom told her he was sleeping like a bear, and she could get him up. Pam told her mom to let her daddy know that she was trying to move in the morning, and she needed to get a moving truck. "Tomorrow morning!" her mother said in a shocked voice. "Wow, it seems like we really haven't prepared for it since this week has been a rough one for you and your dad."

"I know, right? Just let him know when he wakes up."

"Okay," her mom said, "but I can call and do that for you. Hello! I can do something besides cook," and she started laughing.

Her mom and dad met at work. She used to do the same thing Pam did, but she had problems with her back, so she had to get early retirement. The company was so good to her that they still paid her the same salary she was making, so the family had money coming in once a week from both parents. They never really struggled, and helped people out in hard times when they needed it.

Pam said, "Okay, Momma. I'm sorry about that. If you do that for me, I would greatly appreciate it."

"I will do it now, and I will see you when you get home. I love you," Pam's mother said to her.

"I love you, too," Pam said back.

The day went by, and Pam got home. Her dad had just gotten up, and he needed all that rest. "Hey, baby, your mother told me what was going on tomorrow. I'm sorry that I was sleep when you called, but I was just so dang tired."

"I know," Pam said. "We both were beat and worn out this week."

"Well, I guess we can get started packing your room up in a minute, me and the kids."

"Okay, I just need a minute to get myself together," Pam said.

"Oh no, baby, not you," her daddy replied, "The rest of us are going to do it and you can just rest."

"Okay, Daddy," she said as she hugged him. "I'm so blessed to have a father—I mean, a daddy—like you." They both started laughing.

"You can lie down in the guest room, and when the food gets finished, I will let you know so that you can eat." Pam got ready for bed early, because she knew it was going to be a long day ahead for her on Saturday. Pam ate, and a second later, she was asleep. She slept all night long, and when the morning hit, she was good to go.

Pam woke up well rested and ready to get started. She walked into her room, and there was nothing in it. "Where is all my stuff?" she said to herself. She walked down the hall, and there was still no sign of anything. She was freaking out, until she opened the garage door and saw all of her stuff in the garage; it was all packed and marked for the movers to pick up. She was just amazed how her family did everything, and she didn't hear a sound while they were moving everything out of her room last night. As she shut the door to the garage, once again, her family amazed her. They were all dressed and ready to help out with the moving. Pam couldn't hold it in any longer: the overwhelming support from her family was simply amazing, it overpowered her.

"Well, my firstborn, it's time. You ready?" her dad asked.

"Yes," she replied as she wiped her tears. "Yes, Daddy, I'm ready."

Just as she said that, the doorbell rang, and it was the moving people. They were right on time, and ready to get going. They packed up the truck and started on their way to the apartment. The manager was just pulling in when they arrived, and the owner was there as well. They pulled up to the front office.

CHAPTER THREE

"THE OWNER INTRODUCES HIMSELF"

"Hello, everyone," the owner and manager said to the family. "I see that you all are right on time this morning."

"Yes, we are, and ready to move in so we can get these movers off the clock. They are charging by the hour," Pam's dad said. "Let's get moving!"

Everybody started laughing. The manager got the keys, but it was a different unit. This one was closer to the front of the building. The owner told Pam that he felt that since she was young, she needed to be closer to the security people so they could respond more quickly if anything happened. They hoped it wouldn't happen, but just in case, it was easier to get to her.

"Well, thank you," her daddy said to the owner, and shook his hand as they proceeded to the apartment. They walked into the apartment and her mother, brother, and sister thought it was really nice.

Her brother was like, "My sister got it going on in this apartment. I really like this."

Pam only had her bedroom suite, and she was going to buy everything else later. As the movers finished, the owner said, "That all the furniture you have?"

Pam said, "Yes, for now."

The owner said, "We are about to redesign the model apartment. You can have anything in there you like if you want it."

Her family was like, "Dang, you sure are a nice man."

"Hey, I am very proud of this young lady. She took what she heard in what she knew God had for her without waiting to see if God really told her that. So, with that, God makes people be in the right position at the right time, and this is the right time for her."

"Amen," her daddy said to the owner. The owner even helped pay the movers to move the things that Pam wanted to her home. Her parents started to get concerned about why he was doing all of this stuff for their daughter for really nothing.

As they wrapped up everything, the owner told them goodbye, and he hoped everything worked out. Pam's dad said to him, "We do appreciate everything you have done for our eighteen-year-old daughter," with a curious smile on his face.

"Hey, anytime," the owner said.

"Well, we're done, and I'm so happy I did it," Pam said.

"You glad to be away from your family? Is that what you are saying?"

"No, Mama, I'm just saying I feel independent now; nothing negative."

Her mother said, "Okay, just checking, because we've never seen a man so eager to help somebody so much for nothing, and I know that nothing in life is free. It never has been, and it never will be. You just remember that."

"Mother, what are you talking about?" Pam asked with a confused look on her face.

"I'm just saying it is just strange for somebody to do all of this for nothing. Just bothering me a little bit."

"Oh, my God, Mom, I just met that man with Dad. I have never met or seen him a day in my life," Pam said in a shocked voice. "You think I know him and have done something with him? Is that what you think? Is that what you think of me now? Ya'll think that I'm in a relationship with him because he did this for me? Wow, I'm really shocked at ya'll. Dang, what is going on with ya'll?" Pam started to cry, because that really hurt her feelings. She was really a virgin, as she had almost never been intimate with anybody, just foreplay, because she really wanted to save herself for the right person, or marriage. When her parents really saw that she was hurting, they told her that they were sorry and they had just jumped to conclusions. They should know better than to think that a wonderful person like her would ever do something like that. As they told her to calm down, she took a deep breath and said, with a little giggle as she wiped her tears, "Yeah, I can see that you would think something like that when this man has never met me. It would look suspicious to me if I were a parent. So, I'm okay." They hugged, went to go get some food, and then brought it back to Pam's house to eat.

As the night was about to come to an end, Pam's parents asked if she was going to stay at her place or come to their home tonight. She said that she would sleep in her own bed and get used to being by herself for a change, so they hugged her and told her that if she needed anything, to just call them and they would be right there. They only lived about five minutes away from her, so it would be no problem getting to her fast.

That night, Pam went to sleep in her new home with no problem. When she was asleep, her phone started ringing, but she thought she was dreaming or something. Then, she realized it really was ringing. She answered in a sleepy voice. "Hello?"

"Did I wake you?" the other voice said.

"Who is this?" Pam asked.

"It's Peter. I'm the owner of the apartment. I forgot, I never told you my whole name, because on my card, it just has my last name."

Pam replied, "Okay, is something wrong?"

"No, no, no, everything is fine. I just wanted to know if you were going to church this morning."

Pam was very tired, and had had a really long week, so she told him no. "I'm kind of tired, and I really wanted to just relax and get my mind together."

"Oh, I see. Don't let me stop you from your rest. I got to go and thank God for everything you've done for me this week."

At this time, Pam was feeling kind of guilty, so she said, "I would go, but I don't have a car to get there. I will ask my parents next time."

"That's no problem. I also have an apartment here in the complex, so I don't have to drive home and be ready for Sunday," the owner said.

"Oh, okay. Well if you come get me, I will go."

"That will be fine," the owner said. "I can be there in 40 minutes, if that's fine with you?"

"That's fine," Pam said. "See you then."

"Okay bye."

Pam got up, dragging, but she knew she had to go with Peter because of what he had done for her. She remembered what her parents had told her, that nothing in life was free. So, she got ready, and just like he said, in 40 minutes, he was there. She got in the car, and Peter said, "Good morning."

Pam replied in a happy, but tired voice, "Good morning to you, too."

"Thank you for coming with me to church today. That really means a lot to me," Peter said.

"Oh, it's no problem. I need to pay my tithes, anyway," Pam said as they both laughed. As they headed to church, they were just having small talk with each other until they arrived. Peter jumped out of the car to open the door for Pam. She said *thank you*, and they went in. The service was great. As they left, Pam said, "He really did preach today."

"Yes, he did. I liked it as well." Peter asked if she was hungry. She really was, and she knew she didn't have anything in her house yet.

"Well, I don't want to put you through any trouble," Pam said.

"No, no trouble at all. We can go get some breakfast and you can go home and get your rest," Peter said to her, while smiling as he drove to get some breakfast. They ate and had a nice time. They got home, and once again, Peter opened the door for her and said, "Thank you for a great Sunday, again."

"That's sweet. You're welcome, and thank you for taking me to church with you and feeding me, because I was hungry," Pam said, as they both laughed.

He held out his hand to shake hers, and said, "Enjoy the rest of your day, and I will see you when I see you."

Pam walked toward her apartment. "Okay, bye." She turned around and waved. She went into the house and just threw herself across the bed. "Boy, I'm beat," she screamed. She kicked her shoes off, and before she knew it, she was knocked out.

After sleeping for four hard hours, her phone rang again. This time, it was the front security guard letting her know that she had guests. It was her family. She said, "Let them in." She dragged to the door, saying in a sluggish voice, "I'm never going to get any sleep around here today."

She opened the door, and her mom was like, "Where you been? Did you go out last night or something?"

"No, Mother, I went to church, but I didn't take off. What's up?" She was so tired, she really didn't want to go through explaining everything, but she knew what she was in store for. "Who took you to church? You don't have a car, so somebody had to take you."

"Peter came and got me," she said.

"Peter? Who in the heck is Peter?" her dad asked.

"He is the owner," she said as she flopped on the couch and lay to the side.

"See, I told you he was up to something," said her dad. "I knew it. I knew it. You can't pull that stuff on me."

"No, Daddy, he just called me this morning and asked if I would go to church with him. Dang, man, that's it." Pam was so tired that she was talking and everything was coming out of her mouth like crazy.

"Yeah, right! The next thing he is going to want to take you somewhere else, and then try to sleep with you," said her dad.

"Whatever. I'm just trying to get some sleep," Pam said. "That's all I'm trying to do right now."

"Well, we just came to take you grocery shopping."

"Can ya'll please go for me and let me rest," Pam said to her family. "Please."

"Well, okay, get you some rest and we will go for you," her mom said.

"Thank you," said Pam as they walked out the door.

Her brother said, "I still think she done been to a club."

"Shut up, boy," Pam cried out to him. "I went where you need to be going."

"Yeah, I know – to a club," her brother replied, and went out the door.

Pam was so tired that she just lay on the couch that Peter gave her and went to sleep. Pam finally woke up to realize that she'd slept all through the night. She was just so tired. *Wow! It's 3:00 a.m. How did I do that?* She got up, looked around, and she noticed that she had food like bread, cereal, and spices on the counter. When she opened the refrigerator, she saw that it was full, and her parents even brought her a microwave. "Man, I got some great parents," she said. Knowing that she had to get up in a couple of hours, she had to make sure she set her alarm clock, so she just got out of her clothes and slept for two more hours. Then, she got up and went to work, but the problem was that she was on the same schedule she used to have at her parents' home instead of her new home. She realized that the bus was already gone, and that her dad would make her late, but that was her only choice at the time. As she turned around to walk back to her home, she saw a light; a car was coming towards her. It was Peter. He slowed down, rolled down his window, leaned over, and asked Pam if everything was all right? She told him that she had missed the bus because she was still on her parents' home schedule.

"Oh, okay," Peter said. "Well, do you want me to take you?"

"No, that's okay. You have done so much for me already; I couldn't ask for nothing else," Pam said.

"Oh, no problem at all," Peter told Pam. "I was going to the gym, and it won't be a problem." So, she got in the car and he took her to work. "Have a good day," Peter said to Pam.

"Same to you, Peter," Pam said as she got out of the car. Then, she turned back in shock, and said, "I'm so sorry for calling you Peter."

"Oh, that's okay. You're fine."

"Okay. Well, thanks again for bringing me to work, and I will find out my bus schedule to see what time the bus comes in the morning."

"Okay. Anytime you need me and I can help, I will," Peter said as he started to pull off.

Pam started walking into the building, but something came over her. She started waking in a different way, like sexy. *Oh, my God, I wonder if he is looking at me twist,* she was saying in her head. She slowly turned around in a sexy way, only to look and find no one there. Peter had already pulled off. She was embarrassed, but it was good that no one saw her having her moment. When she opened the door, however, another hand came on it.

"Let me get that for you." It was the janitor. He was cleaning up outside and saw Pam's every move. She was so much caught up in trying to show Peter how she looked that she didn't notice him working in the front.

"Thank you," Pam said to him.

"No problem at all." Her face turned red, but she smiled and kept walking.

The workday was about over, and Pam was wrapping things up. Her co-worker asked how the apartment was coming along. Pam said, "Everything is going great. I got my entire apartment furnished for free."

"Wow! How did you get that?"

"Well, I bought my old bedroom set, and the owner of the apartments gave me my living room, dining room, lamps, and pictures for free."

"Dang, girl, what did you do to get that? You must have given him a little taste or something to make him give you all of that," said the co-worker.

"No, he is just a really nice person and he just saw what I had and offered it to me."

"I hear you, girl," said the co-worker. "Get it, girl."

"Whatever, girl," Pam said. She walked out to catch the bus. "Hi, John," Pam said as she got on the bus.

"Well, hello stranger," John said to Pam. "Long time, no see." He started laughing as she took her seat on the bus.

"I'm sorry," said Pam. "I moved, and I was still on my old schedule, but I'm good now."

"So, how you like it so far?" John asked.

"Well, so far, so good. It's only been a couple of days, but everything is fine." As the bus was driving, Pam had to go past her parents' home, where she stood up, and then realized that this was no longer her stop.

Looking in the rearview mirror, John just shook his head and started laughing. "Baby girl, you are going to be alright as long as you're riding with me. I will make sure you get home safely."

Pam, being embarrassed, just crossed her legs and put her hand across her face. Soon, she reached her place and got off the bus. "I will see you tomorrow morning, early. Not at your parents' home time, but earlier than that," John said as Pam got off the bus.

"Okay, I will be here tomorrow on time," she said. As she was walking, she was saying, "This has been a long day."

She made it in, and kicked her shoes off, rubbed her feet, and just sat on the couch for a minute. She closed her eyes for a minute to meditate, and then she jumped back on her feet. Her parents called to check on her, and she told them that everything was fine and that Peter had to take her to work.

"What did he do, spend the night?" her mother asked in a suspicious voice.

"No, he didn't. I was on ya'll house's time instead of changing the time to where I am now. Peter was going to the gym and asked if I needed a ride. Man, you are really freaking me out with this."

"It is just ironic that this man gave you everything, then turns around, and by luck, he is up and ready to go to the gym when you have to go to work. That right there sounds like a stalker to me. Just be careful about him. I got this feeling that's inside that needs to come out about him. Something ain't right. I can feel it," said her mother about Peter.

"Mom, that feeling that you have is called gas," Pam said in a sarcastic way. "If you been feeling that way all day, maybe you need to take some kind of medicine to blow all of the hot air out of you and you will feel much better."

"Look, honey, don't get smart with me. I'm just looking after your safety," her mother said.

"Just keep praying for me and my safety, please. I love you, but I really got to go. Give everybody a hug for me, okay?" She was trying to rush her mom off the phone because she didn't want to hear all that mess she was talking.

"I will, honey. You just be careful there," Mom said.

"Okay, Mom. I gotta go. Bye." She hung up the phone and made a gesture, saying, "They are getting on my nerves with this." As she was walking towards the kitchen, she said, "I wonder what they bought me yesterday." As Pam looked through the cabinets, she saw that her parents had loaded her up with food. "Oh wow! They really hooked me up at the store." Pam had never really seen what they bought at the store, since she was so tired from the weekend. She called her parents to thank them, because they really looked after her, and she started to feel bad about how she rushed her mother off the phone.

"Hello?"

"Hi, Mom. I just wanted to say thank you all for all the food ya'll brought me yesterday. I just really saw what ya'll had brought me and I just want to say thank you."

"You are welcome," her mother said to her, "and let me not hold you up."

"Mother, I'm just really trying to get comfortable in this new environment. It kind of scares me when you and Dad talk like someone is out to get me. I just really want peace and happiness in my life, and drama-free, like it has been in my life. Okay?"

"Well, I understand, and I apologize for saying all those things I said earlier. Can you forgive me and your father for being overprotective?"

"Yes, Mother, you know that. Let me make something to eat so I can get ready for work. I love you!"

"I love you, too, baby," Pam's mother said to her as they hung up the phone.

Pam ate some dinner, laid out her clothes for work, watched a little TV, and went to sleep. She woke up on time, got to the bus stop, and had a wonderful day at work. In fact, the whole entire week went great, so when she got home from work Friday, she was just speaking and talking to everybody around her. She even spoke to the security guards instead of just waving to them. "Hi, guys. How has ya'll's day been going?"

"Fine. We just been patrolling the lot," they said back to her.

"Well, ya'll are doing a very great job. Keep up the good work."

"Thanks for that," one security guard said to her, "and have a wonderful weekend."

"Wow! Thanks," she said, "and ya'll do the same." As she was walking toward her home, she saw Peter out front at the office with a woman. She started to get jealous for no reason, looking at him and trying to see if it was someone special to him. As she got closer, Peter looked up and saw Pam. He asked her how her day went, and was everything fine at the apartment. "Yes, everything is wonderful," she said, "and how was yours?"

Peter replied, "Long, but it was pretty good as well."

"Okay, well I will talk to you later," Pam said to him as she went into her apartment. "Wow! I'm tripping. I was a little jealous just then. Wow, this is like crazy. I need to just chill." She walked into her house, kicked her shoes off, and just started to relax. All of a sudden, her phone rang and it was Peter. "Hello?"

"Hi, it's me, Peter."

"Hi," Pam said.

"Well, I was wondering if you would like to go out for dinner with me after I finish talking to my agent who is handling my business overseas for me."

"No, I don't mind," Pam said.

"Okay, give me about 20 minutes and I will be there."

"Sounds great," Pam said as they hung up the phone.

Pam ran and freshened up her body, then changed clothes. When she got into the car, Peter was looking at her and said, "Wow, you look great, but really, you could have kept on what you were wearing. It was nice, too."

"No, I wanted to change because I've been in that all day," she said.

"Okay, whatever makes you feel better is fine with me."

As they were pulling into the restaurant, her phone rang. It was her parents' home calling, but she knew how they jumped to conclusions, so she let it go to voicemail and turned her phone on silent as they entered the restaurant. They had a great time at dinner, then went and got some ice cream for dessert on their way home. As they pulled up to her complex, she told Peter she had a lovely time, and thanked him. "You're welcome. I just wanted to show you that I like your style about life."

"What do you mean by that?" Pam asked.

"Well, I see that you are a hard worker, and when you want something, you go out and make it happen. So, I really respect a person who is a go-getter in life, not waiting on someone or something to make it happen for them. You understand?"

Pam said, "Yes, I do, and thanks for just making me smile even more now."

"Well, it's the truth," Peter said to her.

"Well, let me get going," Pam said.

"Okay, Pam, have a good one, and if you want to go to church and need a way, just call me. In fact, if you need anything, you still just let me know, okay?"

"Okay," Pam said to Peter, "and goodnight."

"Goodnight Pam; sleep tight," Peter said as he pulled off.

At this time, Pam was on cloud nine, just saying, "He could be the one for me. Oh, let me stop. Let me stop." Pam took off her clothes and just started relaxing. Then, she jumped up and grabbed her purse. She reached into her purse to get her phone, because she was having so much fun that she forgot that she put it on silent. She looked and saw that she had over 50 missed calls. She pressed them to see what she already knew, but before she could do anything, the doorbell rang. She put a housecoat on and peeped through the hole. Oh no, it was the police and her parents.

She opened the door, and her parents said that they came by the house earlier and they thought something was wrong. "We saw your light on and that's why we knocked."

"I'm fine," Pam said.

The police said, "Are you sure?"

"Yes," Pam said.

"You mind if we check the house?"

"Yeah, you can check it." Pam was so embarrassed that she was just stiff. She couldn't talk or move. It was just like all the life went out of her, because it seemed like everybody in the entire complex came out to see what was going on. The police checked and found nothing.

He said, "Since everything is fine, I'm going to leave now." At this time Pam asked her parents if they could leave as well; she needed to have a moment to herself, and she would call them tomorrow.

"Baby, we were just scared, that's all. We just wanted to know that you were safe," her father said to her.

"I know, but can ya'll just call me tomorrow, please," Pam begged.

"Well, we will go, and we are so sorry for caring so much for you. Goodbye."

Pam shut the door. She was so angry and embarrassed that she didn't do anything but go to her room and go to sleep, thinking in her head that this would be over in the morning. She just wanted to sleep on it.

CHAPTER FOUR

"WHO DO I TRUST"

The next morning came. Pam got up and looked out the window to see the sun shining and also to see if anyone was outside. She went in the kitchen and prepared herself some breakfast, then watched some TV. She was trying to forget what had happened the previous night. As she was eating and watching TV, she forgot what was going on around her and started really enjoying what was on TV. Then, all of a sudden, the doorbell rang. It was Peter. "Hello," she said as she opened the door.

"Hi. Are you okay?" Peter asked Pam as her demeanor changed.

"I'm just fine, and you?" she asked Peter.

"Well, I'm just fine now since you are. I came around last night, but I didn't want to be nosey like I'm being now and see what was going on with you, so I asked the police officer what was going on and he told me. Why didn't you tell your parents where you were going?" Pam didn't answer Peter. "Well?" Peter said.

"Well what?" Pam replied.

"Why didn't you tell them that you were with me last night and we just went to go get something to eat?" Peter said in a concerned and confusing tone.

"I forgot," said Pam "I was having so much fun with you and I just forgot to call them, but I feel like I don't have to tell them my every move, you know?" Pam said to Peter.

"I know, but you have to understand that you just moved over to these apartments. You're young, you're by yourself, and you are their first-born. They don't want anything to happen to you. That's what I'm thinking," he said.

"Well, it's more than just that," Pam said.

"Well, what else, then, so I can at least try to help you with it?" said Peter.

"You can't," Pam said. "You can't because they don't care for you, since you must know. Dang, but I like you and I want them to like you, too." Pam started to cry and Peter was shocked at what he had just heard from her about how her parents felt about him.

"Well, do you want me to talk to them? Or better yet, I need to talk to them, because they got it all wrong about everything. Look, Pam, I really like you a lot, and I feel like there is something there, but I really like what you are doing with your life as a whole. You are beautiful, and you are not depending on anyone but God to help you. You're a hard worker. You get up every morning and go to work without somebody telling you to get up and do something with your life. You have a great spirit in you that some people probably can't see because they are too busy looking at your outside beauty. I really wish that your parents could understand that I would never do anything to hurt or use you in any kind of manner of any sort."

"I know you wouldn't do that to me, Peter," Pam said. "I can feel your warmth inside of me that you really are a generous person that is only trying to be a good person, and I do like you. You are a handsome man. You have a great sense of humor. You keep me laughing, and most of all, you are a man of God, which I thought my parents would love. You own your own apartment, but it will always be something, I guess, and my parents just don't get it. They try their best to look for the negative instead of making a positive effort to find good in a person and trusting people, not judging them without any cause."

"I agree one hundred and ten percent," Peter said to Pam. "We never give each other chances because of judging someone or something. No one is perfect in life; no one. The only one that is of that caliber is my lord, God, and he will be the only one in life that is perfect."

"Amen!" Pam said to Peter. "Well, don't worry about them. I will take care of them. Trust me on this, okay?"

"I just want to be of help," Peter said to Pam. "I don't want any problems between me and your parents. I just want them to get to know me a little better than what they think they know."

Pam said to Peter that she would call her parents over and they could sit down and really get to know each other. Peter said, "Not now."

"Why not?" said Pam.

"Because you don't even really know me," he said, as Pam stood there with this surprised look on her face.

"Wow! All right then, I guess I don't, huh?" Pam said.

"No, you don't. I'm not trying to be funny, but you just really know me from around here. In fact, you don't even know my apartment number where I stay in here. You don't know if I'm married or even dating someone. You don't know if I have any children or nothing." Pam still had a shocked look on her face as Peter told her these things. "I really want you to get to know me and tell me if it is really who you would want to be with for the rest of your life."

"Dang, the rest of my life? You are asking me to think about a lot in a short time," Pam said.

"Think about what?" Peter asked.

"You know, about a relationship," Pam said.

"Relationship? Who said something about a relationship?" Peter said in a strong tone.

"You asked if this was something that I would want for the rest of my life. I thought you were talking about us," Pam said in a concerned tone.

"No, I'm saying that for anyone to be interested in someone, don't you think that you really need to find out that person's likes and dislikes in life before it's cupid striking you with the arrow and leading you to destruction?" Peter said.

"Well, of course I would," Pam said to him. "Who wouldn't?"

"That's why I like you. Stay on it and take your time so you don't make the wrong choices in life."

"You're right," Pam said. "So, do you have any of those things you named early? Babies, baby mamas, wives, anything?" Pam asked.

Peter started laughing and said, "It is for me to know and for you to find out."

"Okay, we are a little old for guessing games now," Pam said.

"You're right. No to all the above that you asked me. You think I would do something like that?"

"I don't know what you would do," Pam said. "You put it out there that I need to see who you are and if you're true. I can't say you didn't warn me."

"No, baby girl, I'm single and kid-free."

"Okay."

"But that's why you need to get to know me better, okay?"

"Okay," Pam said.

"Well, now we've got all that out the way, I was really just checking on you, Pam, and I hope that you have a great day today."

"Same to you." As they said goodbye, Pam said, "Oh, by the way, when will I find out where you stay?" She had a little grin on her face.

"Whenever you want to," Peter said, walking backwards.

"Well, I might just call you later," Pam said.

"That's fine by me. Just call me and I'll be there."

Peter turned back around and started walking. "I will do just that," Pam said. "Talk to you later, then," Pam hollered out to him.

"I'll be waiting." Pam went in the house. She was feeling much better now. As the day went by, she cleaned up, then talked to her parents and cleared up everything with them, telling them from now on, she would let them know when she was going out or let them know her whereabouts. The night had come so fast, when Peter called and asked her whether she would go to church with him, and she said that she would.

The next morning came and they went to church, out to breakfast, and then home. Peter kept going when they got to the apartment complex, and went past Pam's to his, so she saw where he stayed. It was very nice. It was almost like a woman stayed in it as well. He took her home that evening and they chatted on the phone for a while, then ended the day with each other. The next morning, Pam was off to work again and she seemed to be on track like she used to be at her parents' home.

A couple of months went by and she was getting to know her neighbors in the complex. It was very peaceful and nice. No crimes at all. There weren't many kids that stayed in the apartments in the first place, so no loud music or all the noise from a kid or teenager. Peter and Pam were still doing the same thing as far as going out to eat, to church, and to different places, which her parents now knew.

One day after church, Peter asked Pam if she wanted to ride with him somewhere. Pam said, "Where are going first?"

"Don't you trust me?" Peter said.

"Yeah, but I would still like to know, if that is fine with you?" she said to Peter.

"Baby, I just want to show you something. Just trust me, okay?"

Pam paused, then said, "Okay, let's go."

They got in the car and drove about 30 miles from where they lived. At the time, Pam was looking a little worried, because Peter made a turn down a single narrow street that went down, then came up. When the car went over a hill, Pam's eyes got big, and she covered her mouth in amazement. She had never seen anything like this in her life. "What is this?" she asked Peter.

"This is my house. Yes, my home. I thought it was time for you to know where my other house was." Pam had only seen something like this on TV and in magazines, but never in person. "Well, are you going to get out?" Pam was in a daze at the time, so she didn't hear Peter when he asked her if she was going to get out. "Hello? Can you hear me?" Peter said to Pam.

"Oh, wow, huh? What did you say?" Pam replied.

"Are you going to get out of the car?" Peter asked.

"Yeah! Yeah! Yeah! Yeah!" Pam said. She couldn't believe her eyes. This is all yours?"

"Yes, it is," Peter replied as they approached the door. His butler opened the door for him. At this time, Pam was in a world of amazement. This man had fish tanks in the foyer walls, elevators, a pool, a movie theater, and a bowling alley. Everything you could think of at his house. "This is so amazing," Pam said.

"You like it?" asked Peter.

"I love it!" Pam said, "And nobody stays here with you?"

"Not at all," Peter said. "This is my little love nest," Peter said as he started laughing.

Pam said, "I think not."

As they drove back home, she couldn't wait to tell her parents, girlfriends, hell, everybody she knew. She talked herself to sleep. When she woke up, it was time for work. She had a wonderful day at work. As the weeks and months went by, Pam and Peter were becoming close friends, and everybody around the apartment complex knew it, too. But the strangest thing was that they had never kissed, never went to the level of being intimate with each other or anything of the sort. Everybody, even her parents, thought that they were doing something of that nature, but Peter never tried, and Pam never tried to seduce him. They were just two people that really enjoyed each other's company. His friends would meet Pam and say to Peter, "I know you be all up in that," and Peter would tell them he hadn't even kissed her.

The same was true for Pam. When she took him places or to little family get-togethers, people would say, "Girl, I know that you be wearing him out," but Pam would tell them that they were just friends, and they hadn't even kissed yet, and her girlfriends and family would ask if he was gay or something. She would tell them that he was just a gentleman, and when the time was right, she felt that she would be ready. One thing about them both–you couldn't try to talk to either one of them while the other one was present, because they had that much respect for each other.

As time went by, they really started to let the outsiders get to them. They were more touchy feely than ever. They finally kissed, and both enjoyed it. They would roll on each other, but had never gotten to the big show. One day, Pam went to his home and went swimming. The mood was right, and they were kissing. All of a sudden, Pam's top was off, and she was just going with the flow of things. Then, somehow, some way, she was nude and lying on the side of the pool. At this time, Peter looked at her body and told her how beautiful she was. As Peter went for the ultimate, her phone rang. She tried to ignore it, but they got distracted, and the mood was gone. She ran to the phone. "Hello?" she said in a tired voice.

"What are you doing?" It was her mother.

"Nothing, Mother. What's up?" Pam said.

"I hope I didn't interrupt anything," her mother said in a peculiar voice.

"No, you didn't," Pam said in a hyped but mad tone.

"Well, let me let you go then, since you got an attitude. Bye!" And her mom hung up on her.

At this time, everything had left the both of them. Peter said, "Let's just go and let me take you home before they call the police again." Peter was kind of mad and getting tired of her family, and Pam could sense it. The ride home was cold and quiet. Peter pulled up to Pam's apartment and let her out. Not waiting for her go inside, he just sped off in anger. Pam was kind of hurt, but she understood why he was upset. However, still she thought he should have waited for her to get in the door or something. Pam went into the house and went to bed.

The next day came, and Pam woke up and said, "Wow, I really did sleep well." She checked the clock. It was 11:30 a.m. on Sunday morning. "Wow! I missed church with Peter," she said. "He probably called and I didn't even hear the phone ring," but when she checked her phone, nobody had called her. Pam couldn't believe that the man she had fallen head over hills for was mad at her for the first time since she had known him. Pam sat on her couch and started to cry, and asked herself, "Why me? I thought I was a good person. I thought that I showed that to him, and that I really wanted to be with him, but after all this time, all he wanted to do was sleep with me. Why did he wait so long to try something if that's all he wanted from me? It just doesn't make sense to me."

As she continued to cry, she just got up and lay across her bed. She called her mother and told her that she and Daddy were right about Peter. She told them that they were together last night and that it was about to happen, and that when her mom called, they stopped. "After that, he got angry and brought me home, and you know, all this time he would come pick me up for church and he didn't even call or nothing. He went without me this morning," she was crying to them on the phone.

"We told you that he was no good and that he was just trying to take advantage of you. He's probably got a lot of women he has done like this. You are not the first, honey, and you won't be the last," her mother said. She told her that God showed her how this man was, and that church was a front so that Pam would think he was really into the Lord and fall for him. "I knew it! I knew it!" her mother screamed. "Leave that man alone, I say. He is nothing but the devil. Trust me when I tell you to leave him alone," her mother kept shouting to her.

Pam was listening to everything her mother was saying, and her father just agreed with his wife. "Honey, didn't I say last night that man wasn't right and he was up to something? Didn't I say that?"

"Yes, you did," her father said.

"We are on our way over there," her mother said, "and we cooked breakfast, so we will bring you some."

"Okay," Pam said.

They hung up the phone, and Pam had made up her mind by listening to her parents that Peter was only after one thing. So, she went to get ready for the day. Then, the phone rang. She didn't know who it was, because the phone was down. "Hello?" she said.

"Hey," Peter said a sleepy voice, "are you busy?"

Pam said, "No, what's up?" in a mean way.

"What's wrong with you?" Peter asked, as he could tell that her voice was a little hostile.

"Nothing is wrong with me. What's up with you?" Pam said.

"Nothing. I just called to tell you that I had overslept this morning and I'm just getting up, because I have been up all night with my stomach. I think I got a virus or something and I pulled off because I thought I was going to be sick. That's why I was so quiet, trying to concentrate on not letting anything come up, if you know what I mean," Peter said. As Pam listened and was feeling really stupid, Peter told her that he was rushing to get in the house so bad that he had lost the back of his phone and he just found the battery earlier. He said that he wasn't feeling well and he had tried to get some rest, but Pam was starting to feel like he was lying, because she had no calls that morning.

"Well, I don't have any missed calls from anybody this morning," Pam said.

"Well, I thought I left you a message."

Pam, in a sarcastic tone, said, "It wasn't me that you left a message with; maybe someone else, but not me."

"I'll let you go. Just call me when you get yourself together," Peter said, "because it sounds like you got an attitude."

"No, I just said I don't have any missed calls."

"Well, I don't care; I know what I did," Peter said and hung up the phone.

"Yeah, you liar, you just been caught," Pam said. To herself, she said, "I'm going to check my phone anyway, just to prove to him that I'm not a fool and young minded. Matter of fact, I'm going to call him back and put him on three-way with me." She called him back and told him that he was liar and that he was just mad at her about last night.

"What the heck are you talking about?" Peter shouted.

"No, let the truth be known," Pam said. "You just mad because nothing happened like you thought it would and now you are making up some mess just to make yourself look good, and I'm going to prove it right now," Pam said to him.

"Well, prove it then," Peter said in an angry voice.

"Don't be hollering at me," Pam said.

"Man, just do what you are going to do," Peter said to her.

"Well, just hold on," she said as she clicked to the other line and called her voice mail, then clicked him back over as it rang. She entered her password and it said that she had two messages. The first message said just what Peter told her and the second one was that he loved her. She'd made herself out of a fool. "I'm so sorry, Peter," Pam said in a sad voice.

"Oh, I forgot I called you back and left that as well. Goodbye Pam," and he hung up the phone. She had made a complete butt of herself, and just probably lost a good person because of something that wasn't true.

Her parents got there, and Pam was crying once again, because she knew that she let her people get in her head and they had her thinking that way when she was the one that had been with Peter, not them. How could they know him when they were not around him? "They can't know him when I keep telling them things," Pam was saying, as they were coming in the house.

"Hey, honey, we bought you some food." Her mother came in and placed the food on the counter. "Baby, stop thinking about that man and come eat something."

"Mom, ya'll were wrong about him, and I think that I have lost him because of ya'll," Pam said to her parents.

"Us? What did we do, but try to help you?" her mother and father said. "Whatever he is telling you are a bunch of lies."

"No, they're not. He told me that he was sick and that he left me a message telling me that, but instead of checking my phone, I called ya'll and let ya'll talk me into some mess that has probably cost me a great person."

"Well, there are others out there that you can get, honey. Don't even worry about him," her mother said while preparing the food for her. "Now, come over here and eat this food before it gets cold." You can tell that Pam's mother was very controlling and that she wanted everything to go her way, because all her daddy did was agree with her mother, whether she was right or wrong. Her mother would never outright tell anyone that she was sorry for anything she had done wrong. She would let it be, and tell others to just let it go. Pam knew how her mother was, and that she wasn't going to hear anything Pam was trying to say about Peter, so she just ate and talked. When her parents left, she tried to call Peter, but he didn't answer. She left him a message telling him how sorry she was, that it was a misunderstanding of the entire situation at the time, and that they just needed to let it go and start over with their friendship. She hung up the phone, but Peter didn't call her the whole day.

Morning came, and she got on the bus dragging. The bus driver asked her what was wrong, and she looked around and saw there was no one on the bus but them. She told him what had happen, and he told her, "Your family can be your biggest downfall in life if you let them. They do more harm than good to you," said John. He told her about how he was to be this big football star, and he went to one of the top colleges in the whole nation. He said that pro teams were looking at him, and that he was all together. He had a girlfriend that had been with him through all his struggles and misfortunes throughout the entire college run, but his parents wanted him to talk to this other woman that was smart and was going to be a doctor. Her parents had plenty of money; they were well-groomed people, and they looked down on his girlfriend. "They helped me with my work as well as keeping me encouraged in my career. So, listening to my parents, I dropped my girl and started dating the one they wanted me to have instead. I did it right after I signed my contract with the Atlanta Falcons."

"So, what happened to you? Why are you driving buses now?" Pam asked him.

"Well, me and the so-called doctor got married, and she was on drugs real bad. Her so-called rich parents both went to jail for drug smuggling, and we got a divorce, but had the kids. I told you about that. Now, I ain't doing nothing, and the woman I truly wanted is a big-time executive with one of the biggest companies in the world. The funny thing about that is, she never threw it up my face. I saw her out, and she hugged me, then asked me to thank my parents for her. I said, 'Thank them for what?' I asked, and she said, 'Because of them, I thought that I was a nobody, but my trust in God made me realize that I was somebody, just around the wrong people,' and I didn't catch it until she pulled off in a brand new sports car.

"See, you can't let people run your life. We are all put here for a reason, and that reason is to fulfill what God had for you when you came out of your mother's womb. Don't let others tell you what they want you to do. Do what God tells you to do, because ten times out of ten, God is always, without a doubt, right. Don't let your family run your life. Trust me, you will end up unhappy. I know what I'm talking about. I should've, could've, would've, and like me, it may be too late."

"It probably already is for me," said Pam.

"No, you're still young. You are at that age where you've got time to change things and make it work for you."

"Thanks so much, John." As she left the bus, she hugged and kissed John, and went to work.

Everything ended up going great at work for her, as well as her ride home. As she was walking home, she saw Peter. He stopped his car and got out. She ran up, and before he could say anything, she gave him a big hug and a kiss. "I'm so sorry. I promise you our friendship will just be ours, okay?" she said to him.

He looked in her eyes and said, "That's why I stopped it. If I'm going to walk with God, then I've got to learn to forgive people and let God handle the situation, not me, because it goes to show that whatever I know ain't true shouldn't bother me, not one bit. I know who I am and where I'm going in life, so that's that. Let's go and get something to eat, okay?"

"Okay," Pam said.

Her night went great, and that night, Peter spent the night with Pam. The passion was all in the hold that they had on each other as Pam tucked her body into Peter and they went to sleep. They woke up, and he took her to work, then went to the gym. The friendship was back.

CHAPTER FIVE

"A PART OF ME"

As time went by, Pam and Peter would only roll around on each other, just foreplay, but one day, Peter just went for it. However, Pam didn't want to yet. "What's wrong?" Peter asked.

"Nothing, I'm just not ready."

"Dang, girl, how long will it be? It has been what, almost a year or so, and we have been good to each other. Don't you want to?" Peter said as he tried to push her back down on the bed, but Pam fought him off.

She said, "No. I mean no."

"Baby, you just been using me all this time to get what you wanted," Peter said to her in an angry voice. "You are going to give me some. You see this?" he said as he opened up his pants. "I'm ready, and I can't leave like this." She had never seen Peter act this way.

He tried once again to lay her back on the bed, but Pam started to fight harder and screamed, "Stop!" louder.

At this time, Peter got up and said, "You are a little tease, but I'm done with you and your games you playing. I'm out." Peter pulled his pants up and stormed out the door. Pam just lay there in the bed. She knew that she couldn't call her parents, so she just laid there and went to sleep.

The next day it stormed really badly. She got to work and out of all days, it was inventory time. The day went by slowly, and it was hailing so badly that when she ran to the bus, she almost fell. She was soaked, and it was night because they had to work overtime, and the clouds made it really dark. When she got off the bus, she ran home.

She was so tired that she dropped her keys when she unlocked her door. As she bent down to get them, someone pushed her inside her apartment. The person locked the door. He had on all black from head to toe. His voice was so low and deep that Pam couldn't even try to scream, because he said if she did, she would be sorry. He ripped her clothes off in a way that she couldn't do anything. Tears were running down her face, but all of her power had left her. She was lifeless as the person entered in where no man had been before. His body was on top of hers, and it seemed like forever. All of a sudden, the person started shaking, and holding Pam tight, but not hard. Then, he got up and left. What just happened? Nothing came out of her mouth. She couldn't even talk or move. Her phone rang, and she couldn't answer it; she was numb.

She lay in the same position for about 20 minutes and finally realized what had happened. She screamed as loudly as she could, "Help me! Somebody! Please help me. Help me! Help me! Oh, my God, somebody please!"

The neighbor across the hall was coming home, heard her, came in, and called the police. The sweet young girl that was good to everybody had been raped. She saw her life change that fast, right in front of her eyes. "Lord, what did I do to deserve this? What did I do, Lord? Please tell me," she cried out to him. "Why did you let this happen to me? I did what you told me to do. Why did you punish me like this?" They took her away in an ambulance.

Her phone was ringing, and it was her mother. "Hello? Who is this?" her mother said.

"This is the police. Who are you?"

"I'm her mother. I mean Pam's mother. Is this her phone?" she asked the police.

"Yes it is. We are taking her to the hospital."

"For what?" her mother said.

"It seems like she has been raped." Pam's mother dropped the phone and fainted.

Pam's father ran by her, and then picked up the phone up. "Hello? Hello?" he screamed.

The police told him to calm down, but he needed to listen. "Okay," her father said.

"Now, who are you?" the police asked.

"I am Pam's father. What is wrong?" he asked

"Well, your daughter has been raped," the police said.

"What the hell do you mean she been raped?" the father said.

"Sir, can you please calm down. We are taking her to the hospital to get her checked over. She is in route right now to the hospital, okay? You can go there and they will give you more information about her condition."

Pam's father tried to get his wife up. She finally came to. They rushed to the hospital to see their daughter. Once in the hospital, they started to panic, and were just asking anybody how to get to where people were taken that had been raped. Finally, someone knew, and they rushed down the hall. There she was—lying on the bed, lifeless. They ran over to her bedside as tears just start coming down Pam's face, but still, she lay motionless. Her daddy just fell to his knees and started praying right at her bedside.

Finally, Pam spoke, but only said, "Why?"

"We don't know why, honey, but are you okay?" her father asked.

"What do you think?" Pam said in a way her daddy had never heard her talk before. "How do you think I feel when God only knows who came into my world and took part of my spirit and my soul with him? Huh? Why, when ya'll felt everything else was going to happen? Why didn't no one call to tell me that I was going to be raped? God didn't speak to neither one of ya'll and warn ya'll that someone was going to rape your daughter, since he tells ya'll and warns ya'll of everything else? Tell me, Mother, didn't weird feelings come over you last night? Huh? Out of all the things to hear from God and how God has told you time after time what was going on in my life, you mean to tell me he told neither one of you nothing?"

"Now, young lady, you calm down right this minute, talking about God like you think it's his fault that this happened to you," her mother said. "I know you are hurting and all, but don't talk that way about nobody, especially God."

"Oh, you know how I'm feeling, but you are so funny, Mother. You know everything and how everything supposed to be, but when it is really time to know something, guess what? You don't."

Before Pam's parents could say anything, the doctor came in and asked them to leave, because she was still a little disoriented from the whole ordeal and she needed to get some rest. They told her *goodbye*, and Pam just said, "Bye. Go pray to God and ask him why he didn't warn ya'll that this was going to happen to me."

Her mother started crying, and saying, "Why was she talking like that to us? Why is she so angry at us? Where did we go wrong?"

"I don't know; I really don't know," he said. They sat out in the visitor's lounge and waited to hear anything else from the doctors. At this time, the kids came with a friend of the family's, and they all sat and waited, until her brother went to the desk and asked what was going on and whether she was okay.

"Yes, she is doing okay," the nurse said. "Would you like to see her?"

It was like something was telling him to see her on his own, so he said, "Yes. What room is she in?" The nurse took him to see her, and when he saw his sister in the bed, he almost cried, but he knew he had to hold it together for Pam's sake. "What's up?" he said.

"Nothing much," Pam replied.

"Everything cool with you?" the brother asked.

"Yes, everything cool. What's up with you?" Pam asked.

"The same old. You know how that goes, but since you left, I got your room, so, you know, I'm really living it up now." They both started laughing. They talked and laughed for a while, but the funniest thing was that her brother never talked about what happened to her. He had never even come close to anything dealing with the matter at hand; he just talked like she was at home or something. "Well, baby girl, let me get out of here." He kissed her on the forehead, and when he raised up from kissing her, she grabbed him, hugged him tight, and didn't let him go. He said, "I always got your back, sister. Always. I promise," he whispered in her ear.

"Thank you! Thank you so much," she said as the tears rolled out of both of their eyes. "

"Well, let me go before I get soft on you," her brother said, and they started laughing and wiping their tears away.

As he left the room, Pam said, "I love you."

"I love you, too, girl. Now, get back out here for me," her brother said.

"I will," Pam said.

That was what Pam needed–someone to make her feel good about herself and feel good about life. Pam stayed overnight, and the next day, she was released. Her parents had stayed all night with her. Her father told her job what happened, but it had also made the local news, so her job was already aware of what took place. They took her back to their house, because they thought that it would be best for her instead of going back home. She stayed there for a week, and then said that she had to go back to her house. During this time, Peter did not call once to check on her or anything. Even though they got into it, she still felt like he should have called her. They took her home, and she walked in and told her family that she was fine, and that she wanted to be alone so that she could adjust back to everything.

"You sure? Because I can stay over here with you if you want me to," her brother said. "It would not be a problem at all."

"Now, you know all of ya'll have just been wonderful to me, so now it is time for me to get back on the ball and get going," she said.

"Well, we are here for you, and we got your back," her mother said.

As they walked out the door, Pam saw them leave and rushed to her phone to call Peter, but it went straight to voicemail, and his mailbox was full. She tried three more times later that day, but it was the same. No answer and mailbox was full. As she was sitting there, she thought about their argument and their fight. Then, she thought about what happened the next day. She thought about how all of a sudden, she couldn't reach him. "No. Stop thinking like that, girl," she said to herself. "Okay, let me get up and do something around here fast before I lose my mind." But, for some reason, the thought couldn't be put out of her mind, because it was so strange how everything ended up. Here, she was fighting against a man because he wanted it and she denied him, and then, the next day, a man took what she didn't give to the man who she really thought deserved it. "What if I would have given it to Peter? Would I have been raped?" she asked herself.

As she was sitting on her bed, she was thinking back to the whole rape ordeal. She was thinking that a rape victim is sometimes beaten or there is some type of weapon, but he did none of that. "He was very gentle, not forcing himself in me, and when he got excited, he held me with a passionate hold, not a force-like squeeze or hug. It was like he was being intimate with me, not raping me. I wonder if that was him, Lord." She looked up to the sky for answers from God. "Let me stop tripping," she said. "I know Peter wouldn't even attempt anything of that manner with me. I know he didn't want it that bad, or did he?" Pam just lay in her bed and went to sleep.

The next day, she woke up and went straight to check her phone. There was nothing. Then, she checked her voicemail. Nothing there either. Another week went by with no calls or anything from Peter, so she asked her mother if she could use her car for the early morning service. Her mother told her yes, and brought the car to her.

That morning, she went to church, but Peter was nowhere in sight as she looked all over for him. She went back, and when she came to the security guard, he told her that the front office wanted to see her. She went in and they told her that they were sorry, and that they had added more security to the apartments. As they were telling her this, she asked where Peter was. They told her that Peter had gone out of the country on as business trip, and that he had been gone ever since the incident occurred.

She was like, "Dang, he really out of town?"

"Yes, but we sent a message to a company that can get in touch with him overseas, so when he calls, I will surely tell him to call you."

"Okay," Pam said, and walked out the door. She couldn't believe this man just up and left without a warning of any kind to let her know that he was going out of town, let alone the country. "That just don't add up," Pam was saying to herself as she drove home.

CHAPTER SIX

"TAKING MY LIFE BACK"

As the weeks went by, Pam became dizzy a lot at work. She was also throwing up a lot, like she had a virus of some sort. She was very edgy at times, and became paranoid of her surroundings. One day while sitting at home, she was trying to eat food, but it kept coming up and she was having hot flashes. She called her mother and asked her to come over, because she felt like she needed to go to the hospital right away. Her mom came over and took her to the hospital, and when she got through, she was about to pass out. Neither she nor her mother knew what was going on with her. She was losing weight, and had caught a cold, because the vitamins she was taking kept coming up.

They took her in and told the mother to wait in the visitor's room. Pam had been getting sick ever since the incident occurred. She was not able to eat, was losing weight, and had a cold. Her mother asked the nurse when she came back out what was going on with Pam. "Well, ma'am, we are going to run some tests on her to see what's going on and let you know from there. You just stay calm, and I'll be back shortly." It had been two hours. The rest of the family came to the hospital and waited with her mother.

"We should have never let her move out so soon," her mother said to her husband. "We should have put our foot down and made her stay put, and none of this would have been happening to her or us."

"Calm down. Don't go blaming yourself; just wait and see what they say."

At that time, the doctor came out and told them the news. Pam's mother and the whole family started crying. It was something that they didn't want to hear. During the rape, the man had given something to Pam that was going to change her entire life. And here was a mother watching her little girl change into a woman right before her eyes.

Her brother said, "Life is so unfair to the good people of the world. Out of all people, my sister's life sucks."

"You all can go see her. She is awake." The family knew she had to receive support from them, so they had to not look worried, because that would upset her.

"Hey!" her mother said and hugged Pam.

"Hey, and thank ya'll for coming for me."

"No problem. We are here for you always," her father said.

"I know ya'll are," Pam said.

"So, whatever they told you, we are here one hundred and ten percent. We will take care of you forever, as long is God is willing," Pam's father said.

"I know ya'll will be here for me, so that's why I'm keeping the baby."

"You are?" Pam's mother said.

"Yes, I am," Pam replied. When it happened, the man had also gotten her pregnant, but Pam said, "This isn't this child's fault. This child deserves to live, and they said that for now, it is normal." The family was shocked, but supportive of her decision in the matter. The family stayed a little longer, then they left the hospital. They wanted Pam to stay another day, so they just let her get her rest.

The family got home and ate, and then they all went to sleep. Pam's mother and father were talking the bed about the whole thing. "How and why does she want to keep a child when she is a child herself?" her mother said to her father.

"That, I don't know. I've been trying to figure that one out myself," her father said.

"How is she going to have a baby without even knowing who the father is, and bring that child up without a father period," her mother said. "Honey, you have got to talk some sense into your child, because I think that this is just a little too much for her to handle right now in her young life."

"I agree, and when she gets home and calmed down, I will talk to her about this baby thing," Pam's father said, as they kissed and went to sleep.

Pam came home, and for two weeks now, her spirit had changed for the better. Finally, Peter had called her, too. "Hi, Pam," he said.

"Hi, Peter," Pam said back to him in an excited voice. "What's up with you?" she said.

"I'm sorry it took me so long, but I left my phone back in the U.S. and I don't know your number by heart," he said.

"Oh, that's okay. I just thought it was weird that you just up and left without telling me anything. That isn't like you at all," Pam said.

"I know, right? But my parents are over here. They were on a vacation from country to country, and there was a bad accident. I had to rush out to see about them."

"Are they okay?" Pam asked.

"Not really," Peter said. "They both have been in a coma since I've been here. I'm just trying to deal with it. Then, I heard about you and this is just too much for me right now. I don't know what to do."

"Well, you just worry about your parents. Don't worry about me. I will be alright," Pam said to Peter.

"So, what happened? Did he hurt you or anything?"

"No, he didn't, Peter. I'm doing just fine."

"I'm so sorry that this happened to you, or happened to anybody," Peter said. Pam wanted to tell him that she was pregnant, but she didn't; they just talked and caught up on everything that had been going on with the both of them. Peter did apologize for his behavior that last night they were together. Peter felt really bad about everything that had been going on in Pam's life at this time, and he promised that when he got back, he was going to do something really special for her. She was about to turn 19 in a couple of weeks, so he really wanted everything to be right. As they hung up the phone, Peter told her that he would be back soon, and that he would write her.

"Okay, so you have the address. Just write soon as you can, and take care" she asked.

"Okay, goodbye, Pam," Peter said.

"Goodbye," Pam said.

They got off the phone, and weeks went by. Her birthday came, and her day went great. She had a little party at work, and went out with her parents and friends, but Peter didn't show. When she got home, Peter had sent her a letter, card, and a $2,000 dollar check.

"He really does care about you," her mother said.

"I know he does," Pam told her mother, "and I tried to tell ya'll that, but ya'll wouldn't listen to me."

"Okay, we're sorry, but did you tell him that you were pregnant?" Pam's father said.

"No, not yet, but I will," Pam said.

"When will you tell him? Don't be using people like that, because it will come back on you," her father said.

"I know. I will tell him soon. I mean, I will tell him when I feel the time is right," Pam said.

As time went by, Pam and Peter were talking and writing each other. Peter's parents were still in comas, but he really felt like they could pull through. After seven months, Peter said that he had to come back to handle some business back home. Pam told him that she had to tell him something that was very important, and he needed to listen to her. Peter said, "Just tell me when I see you, because I'm ready to see you, and I want to see the look on your face when you see me to see if your feelings are like you say they are."

"They are, Peter, but I really need to tell you something," Pam said, but Peter didn't want to hear it. He just told her to wait until he got back.

A couple of weeks went by, and Peter called Pam and told her he was back in town. Her family was over at her house with a couple of her friends. "That's great!" Pam said.

"So, what are you doing?" Peter asked.

"Oh nothing; just got a couple of people over."

"That's perfect," Peter said. "Well, can I stop by?" Peter asked in an excited voice.

"Sure, if you want to."

"Girl, you know I want to see you. Stop playing," Peter said. "I am on my way."

"That's fine," Pam said.

They hung up the phone, and Pam told everybody that Peter was on the way, and that he would be there any minute. They waited, and the doorbell rang. Pam's mother opened the door for Peter, and Pam was sitting on the couch. It was not the welcome Peter was looking for, but he just went along with everything. "Hello," he said to her mother.

"Hi. How are your mom and dad doing?" she asked.

"They are still in comas, but I know that they will be fine," Peter said as he walked in and met the people he didn't know. He saw that Pam didn't even get up. Peter finally said, "Don't I get a hug or something?"

"Yes, you do." She got up, but kept the covers over her to hide her stomach, and she made sure that she didn't press up against Peter. Peter felt like something wasn't right. He asked her what was going on. "Nothing is going on," Pam said as everybody looked at her.

"So, are you still mad at me or something?" Peter asked.

"No, nothing like that," Pam said.

"Well, what is it then? It's something."

"Tell him, Pam. Don't treat him like that," Pam's mother said.

"Like what?" Peter said as he looked at Pam.

Pam stood up and took the blanket off to show him she was pregnant. "I'm sorry," Pam said to him.

"You're pregnant?" Peter said in a shocking, hurt, and confused voice. "By who?" he asked.

Pam said, "I don't know."

Peter was so hurt and embarrassed that he didn't know what to do. "How come you don't know who the baby's father is?"

"I got pregnant when I was raped," Pam said.

"So, are you going to keep it?" asked Peter.

"Yes, I am going to keep it," said Pam.

"Wow! This wasn't what I was planning to come back to. Not at all," he said to Pam. "I came back to give you this." He pulled out a little black box with a five-carat diamond ring. "I came back to ask you to marry me, Pam, and you lay this on me?"

"I'm sorry, Peter. I just wanted you to know earlier, but you wouldn't let me tell you," Pam said as she started to cry. Peter didn't know what to say or do in front of all these people that were watching him and knowing that he was feeling terrible inside.

"Well, I will just go now and ya'll can finish enjoying ya'll's little get-together," he said as he walked toward the door.

"So, that's it?" Pam said. "You just going to walk out and run away from me?" Pam was upset at Peter for just not saying anything.

Peter said, "What do you want me to do? Huh? I will call you later," Peter said to Pam as he opened the door.

"You don't have to call me ever," Pam said to him, "and you can stop sending me money every month as well."

"I didn't send you money but one time. It's probably the child's father sending you the money, because it sure as hell ain't me." Peter shut the door and left. Pam's family and friends just stood in silence.

"What the hell just happened?" Pam said. "What just happened in here? That wasn't supposed to just happen." She ran toward the door to try and catch Peter, but her daddy and her brother grabbed her and told her to calm down. Pam was going crazy. "That wasn't supposed to happen!" she kept screaming as she fell to her knees. "Why Lord? What have I done to my life?" Pam cried out.

As her friends began to leave the house to let her have her moment, they rubbed her back and told her everything would be all right. "Just keep praying, and God will fix it for you."

Everything seemed to be going wrong after that little fight with Peter. He went back with his parents, and stopped calling Pam, but Pam said that God made this inside her, and she is going to keep her child. Time went by, and the big day came for her to have what God had intended for her. Her water broke, and she was taken to the hospital. All went well, but when it was time to bring life, God put a twist on things. At that moment, something happened to Pam as she was giving birth. She was dead to the doctors, but God just needed to talk to her for a minute. Five minutes went by, and the baby had stopped coming out. The doctor and nurses were working like crazy to now save them both, and all of a sudden, everything kicked back on. She was alive, and the baby was born. He was a little king. His hair was so beautiful. He had big pretty eyes, long eyelashes, and the funny part was that he didn't come out crying; he came out smiling. They had to make him cry. He was 7 pounds, 5 ounces, and 21 inches long.

Pam saw him and said, "That is my son?" She held him to her breast as she kissed him on the top of his head and said again, "This is my son. He is so beautiful." She was holding him ever so gently as he opened his eyes, looked at her, and smiled. Pam shed a tear and told him, "Mommy will take care of you. I promise you that." She was so protective of him that she didn't even want him to go to the nursery. She wanted him there with her at all times, but they had to take him. Her parents kept a close eye on everything.

A couple of days went by, and the baby and Pam went to her parents' home to stay for a couple of weeks. When they pulled up, they helped her and the baby out of the car and into the house. "I can't believe you named that child Peter," Pam's mom said when they got into the house.

"What's wrong with that?" Pam said to her as they laid him on the bed.

"I guess nothing, but you need to just focus."

Pam got settled in with Peter as they stayed at her apartment after about two weeks. Pam's mother would keep him when she went to work, and when she got home from work, Pam would take over. It was like this for six months. One weekend, Pam and the baby went to the store. It was only a couple of blocks from the house, and Pam said she needed the exercise. It was a beautiful day to be out, and when she got in the store, everybody couldn't stop admiring the baby. He was so cute with those fat cheeks like they were full of food, and his curly hair. Pam felt good as a mom. They left the store and headed home. Peter's little stroller had a cart in the back so that she could put food or whatever in it. They got home and played around with each other for a while, and then they both took naps.

Ever since Peter was born, Pam hadn't had much of a social life, and her girlfriends told her that she still had a life. She was only 19, and living like she was an old woman or something. "Girl, you need to just let your parents keep him and go out with us sometimes," one of her girlfriends said to her over the phone while she was changing his diaper.

"Girl, you know that I try not to bother anybody with my project," Pam said as she finished changing his diaper and picked him up.

"Look here, Pam, now you need to meet somebody," her friend said.

"Like who?"

"You're acting like it's over or something. Live a little."

"Dang! I guess you right."

"Hell, I know I am right, and I got the perfect little spot for you," her friend said as Pam agreed to go out with her.

The next weekend came, and Pam and the girls went out to this club/restaurant. All of Pam's friends, including herself, didn't look their ages at all. So, when it was time to get into the clubs, it was no problem for them. They got into the club and everybody was having fun but Pam. "Girl, what's wrong?" one of her friends asked.

"Nothing. I'm just not feeling this."

"Now, come on. Your baby will be fine. He is with your parents. He can't get any safer than that."

"Yeah, you're right," Pam said as she looked up and saw this man just staring at her and approaching where they were.

"How are ya'll ladies doing tonight?"

"Fine. What's up with you, Kevin?" one of Pam's friends said, because she worked with him at this corporate office downtown. He was one of the top people in the entire company, but the bad side was that he knew he was the truth.

"I'm doing just fine now that I see all this beauty at one table. And who might you be?" He put his hand out to shake hers.

"My name is Pam."

"Pam . . . what a pretty name. Mine is Kevin Griffin. Nice to meet you, Pam," he said as they shook hands. "Can I buy you a drink or something?"

"Well, a Coke would be nice," she said.

"Well, Coke it is. Does anybody else want something?" Kevin asked the other ladies.

"Hell yeah! Get me a gin and tonic," one girl said.

"Get me a martini," and the other wanted rum and Coke.

Kevin ordered, and told the waiter to put it on his tab. As he walked away, the girls said, "Thank you, Kevin."

"Ya'll are more than welcome," he said as he walked off and went back where he was.

"Girl, did you see how he wanted you, Pam?" one of her girlfriends said.

"He just spoke to me, that's all."

"Girl, don't be stupid. He is one of the top dogs at the company. He has his master's degree, he has a sharp crib, and two cars, a Benz and a Range Rover."

"Okay!"

"Girl, go get it, honey, because I've been trying, but failed," she said, as all the girls started laughing. "Hell, somebody needs to break the bank."

"Well, if he asks me for my number, I will give it to him, but I'm not going to chase him or nothing like that," Pam said.

They left the club, and that Monday evening, Pam got a call from her friend saying that Kevin wanted her number.

"For real?" Pam said in a surprised voice.

"Yeah, so do you want me to give it to him, or what?"

"Yeah, you can."

"Good, because I already did. Whew! That was close, but I knew you would say yes." The girlfriend started laughing.

"Girl, you are a trip and wrong for that," Pam said. "Anyway, I will talk to him when he calls and I will see what he's talking about."

"Okay, call me, girl, and let me know, too." Pam and her friend hung up the phone, then Pam gave Peter a little wash up and fed him. Before she could finish, he was knocked out. She laid him in his crib and covered him with a blanket.

Her phone rang, and it was a number she didn't recognize. *Who is that? Oh, that might be him.* "Hello," she said.

"May I speak to Pam," the strong sexy voice said.

"This is she."

"Hey, how are you doing today? This is Kevin."

"Hi Kevin," she said.

"Did I catch you at a bad time?" he asked.

"No, you fine," she said.

"So, what's going on with you today?"

"Nothing; just sitting around getting things together for work tomorrow," she said.

"Well, where do you work?" Kevin said. She told him, and Kevin said, "You aren't that far from where I work, are you?"

"No, I'm really right around the corner."

"Well, what are you doing tomorrow at lunchtime?" he asked.

"Mine is at different times, but I do still get an hour," she said.

"Well, you just call me and let me know, and I'll come get you, because I can leave at any time and take my lunch," he said.

"Okay, I sure will," Pam said. They chatted a little longer, then they got off the phone with each other.

The next day, Pam called him and they went to lunch. They had a nice time and got to know a little about each other, but Pam didn't tell Kevin about Peter, because she felt it was a little too soon for that. They went out on dates without Kevin ever knowing about Peter, because her mom or her girlfriends would always have him.

One night, they went to this restaurant, and Pam told Kevin that she enjoyed his company and she liked being around him. Kevin told her that he felt the same way about her, but Pam noticed that Kevin was kind of cocky and arrogant. So, she didn't want to say anything wrong where it would mess up everything. She just waited to tell him about her child. When they got to her place, he walked her to the door this time. Pam had never let anybody as far as a man come into her place, and she knew Peter was in there.

"Thank you for walking to my door," she said as she was unlocking the door, hoping he didn't ask to come in.

"My pleasure. I was hoping I could see your place," he said.

"Not tonight. Maybe the next time, because I really got to get up in the morning and I just want to lay it down, you know?"

"I understand," Kevin said. "I'll just wait until next time so that you can clean up, I guess."

Pam started laughing and gave him a kiss. "Goodnight, and thank you again," she said as she went inside. "Whew! That was close."

"Girl, what's wrong with you?" her friend asked.

"Girl, he wanted to see the place, and I'm not ready for that right now," Pam said as she went right in to check on Peter.

"Why not?" her friend asked.

"I haven't told him about Peter yet, and I don't know how he is going to react to him."

"Girl, you haven't told him about your child? That should have been the first thing you told him about so that the air would be clear."

"I know, but he is kind of stuck on himself and I don't know if a child is in his world right now," she said.

"Well still, girl, this is part of you. Forget him if he can't accept your child. Hell, he was once somebody's little child, so he can't look down on you or nobody else," her friend said to her as she grabbed her things so that she could leave. "Don't let anybody make you ashamed of you and your child."

"I'm not thinking about nobody when it comes to me and my child. I just feel like he is a little cocky, and I just don't want him to say something out of the way about nothing."

"Well, sooner or later, you got to trust somebody at some time in your life," her friend said as she was walking out the door.

"I am, but this is kind of new to me, and I'm not just going to put myself and my baby out there like that," Pam said.

"Okay, alright, I get you. I will talk to you tomorrow," her friend said and shut the door.

The next day came and Pam got a call at work. "This is Pam. How may I help you?" she asked.

"You can help me by gong to lunch with me," the other voice said.

"Who is this?" she said.

"It's me, Kevin."

Pam got a little upset at him for calling her at her job, because she didn't want anybody in her personal business at all. "Why did you call my job?" she asked.

"Well, I just wanted to ask you if you would like to go to lunch with me."

"Okay, why couldn't you call me on my phone instead of my work phone?"

"Wow, my fault. Boss going to get you or something, because I don't want you to get a beating from him," Kevin started laughing.

"I don't find it funny," Pam said, and hung up the phone on him. He called her on her cell phone, but she turned it on silent. He left her a message saying that he was sorry, and that he didn't mean to get her in trouble. He said he really was sorry, and that he would never call her at her job again. Pam was so pissed that she didn't answer any of his phone calls that whole day.

Pam was a very private person, and she didn't want or like people in her business. So what he did was really striking a nerve in her that was hard to ignore. That night, her girlfriend called her. "What's up, girl? What's going on with you?"

"Nothing," Pam said.

"What's going on with you, girl? Kevin said you are mad at him."

"I am. He called up to my job, and you know I hate that, especially if it is personal," Pam said. "You know, it is just me and my baby, so I try to stay away from all the drama."

"I know, girl, and I understand what you are talking about on that. Why didn't he call your phone?"

"That's what I said, but he said that he really didn't see what the problem was and he made some kind of sarcastic remark, so I hung up on him."

"Well, he told me to tell you that he was really sorry and he will make it up to you."

"Anyway, he just thinks he is the man, but he is not all of that," Pam said.

"Well, I just told you to get the money, you know?"

"I just need to leave him alone, you know?"

"Girl, just calm down and don't jump to thinking negative. It will work itself out the way it needs to."

They hung up the phone and the next morning, Pam was at work when a guy came in with two-dozen roses. Everybody wondered who was getting those. The deliveryman said, "Is there a Pam here?"

"That's me," she said with a confused but happy smile on her face.

"Can you sign here for me, ma'am."

She signed, and read the card. It said, "I'm sorry for acting like a jerk, and if we can just start this over and make this work, I'm yours to keep. Signed, Kevin."

Pam was surprised and thankful. At lunchtime, she called him and they talked for about 10 minutes, and after work he came and picked her up. "So, how was your day?" he asked her as he pulled off from her job.

"It went pretty good today," she said, "and how about yours?"

"Oh, it was cool."

"So, thanks again for the flowers. That was sweet of you."

"No problem. I try to do the right things with the right people," Kevin said. "Would you like to get something to eat?" he asked.

"No, that's okay," Pam said.

"You got time. I picked you up and I can get you home at the same time as the bus does."

"Kevin. I have to tell you something about me before this goes any further."

"What is it?" Kevin asked with a concerned look on his face.

"Well, I have a child. My baby is very special to me, and that's why I didn't let you come in the other night, because I didn't know how you would act by knowing it."

Kevin looked in shock. "Wow, that was something to hit a person with," he said, "but all is well. I can work with that."

"You can?" Pam said.

"Sure, I can. I would love to meet him," Kevin said.

"You would?"

"Yes. Heck, we can see him right now if you would like me to," he said.

"Sure," Pam said. They went to her house where her mom was with Peter, but he was asleep at the time. She introduced Kevin to her mother, and to Pam's surprise, she really liked Kevin. Kevin was only 22, and had been a top person in the company since he graduated from college early with a master's degree after taking college classes early in high school. Her mother was very impressed with his achievements in his life. Kevin told Pam that she had a beautiful home and a beautiful mother, but he better get a move on since Peter was asleep and he didn't want to wake him up.

"Well, Kevin, it was very nice meeting you, and you come back, you hear?" Pam's mother said as Pam walked him to the door.

"Yes, ma'am, I will, and you all have a great evening."

Pam shut the door. "Oh, girl, now I like him. How did you meet him?" her mom asked.

"I met him through a friend of mine. Why are you so concerned all of a sudden about this person who you don't even know that good? Okay, just in a couple of minutes you now all in love with him?"

"Whoa! Where is all this hot air coming from?" her mother said.

"I just don't understand you sometimes, Mama. I had a man that really liked me and was willing to give me everything, but you didn't even give him a chance. Now, you see this dude who is sort of cocky with his attitude, and you head over heels about him. I just don't understand that at all," Pam said as she went to go get Peter, because he had woken up from his nap.

"Now, wait a minute. Hold on now," her mother said. "I'm not head over heels for nobody, and with that Peter thing, yes, I thought he was too old for you at the time and that you were not ready for someone like him in your life. The guy right here is around your age and it looks better when you got a person who is close to you in age so that ya'll can grow together in life."

"Mother, I could, or he could, get real sick. We can die. We can lose at any time in life. What he has is something that can be taken from him at any time, but his heart and his spirit can't be. They can be brought down, but they can't be taken from nobody. Everything in that field can be lifted back up in life."

"So can things you lose. You can get them back plus more than you had before, Pam," her mother said. "Now, maybe I did jump the gun a little, but I just want you to understand that life is a complex thing. You win and you lose at something in life. That's how God has it. You have to lose in order to win with God."

"I don't understand," Pam said.

Her mother was holding the baby and told Pam to sit down and listen, so they sat down on the couch. "Look, when I was growing up, my mother and father had it bad, so I had always said I wouldn't go through the things that they went through in their lives, and neither would my kids. My daddy struggled to keep food on the table, and my mother worked and kept the house in order. When I got older and started really seeing things, I was choosing people for the wrong reasons. I had this guy that I thought was the world to me. He would buy me everything and anything my heart could imagine. I was a little bit older than you, so I traveled. I went to the best restaurants in town at the time. He showed me the best time of my life, but my parents didn't like him because was much older than they liked him to be. So, I didn't listen, and this man told me he had a business that he wanted to start and he wanted us to be a team. All he needed was my social and driver's license. I gave it to him as I worked and put money in my account, but he never told me how we were going to get money. It was always just *trust him.*

"Well, one day, he told me that he had to go out of town on a business deal, and our company was about to blow up. I was so excited about what he said that it never dawned on me that this man had wiped my bank account clean. He told me just to wait until he got back and we was good to go. I went home and told my parents that they had him all wrong, and that him and me were about to be wealthy. My parents looked at me and thought I was crazy. 'Girl, what have you done to make this man tell you something like that?' my mama said to me, but, you know, at this time, I'm on a high so big that I said, 'Don't you worry about it. I got this. I know what I'm doing.' I said it like I didn't have a care in the world anymore. Child, I went to the mall with my girlfriend and was just bragging on how my man and me was going to be so rich. I went into a shoe store to buy these shoes, and the lady said my card had been declined. I said, 'You sure? Run it again for me, please.' She did, and the same thing happened. I was saying to myself that this couldn't be, because I knew how much money I had in the bank and there was no way in hell that this could be right.

"I called the bank and told them what was going on, and gave them my information. They told me that I withdrew all the money and closed my accounts. 'You got to be kidding me,' I said. 'No, you took everything out day before yesterday evening around 4:55.' Now it was starting to make sense to me. That was why he came by that morning.

He knew if I would have checked, I would have seen the money, but instead, I trusted him. I started crying. My friends were trying to calm me down, but I wouldn't have it. I had just gotten everything dumped on me at one time. My biggest concern was how was I going to face my parents? I had just basically told them off and said that they didn't know nothing, but I told them, and they caught the guy. He was a con artist and he had used many other women the same way he used me. So, that's why I stay on you and make sure it doesn't happen to you. It took me a minute to bounce back from that, then I met your father, who went through my emotional torment and mental anger and pain, and stayed with me, even though I took him through pure hell. That's why I will love that man until the day my heavenly father comes and take me home with him."

"Wow! Mom, I'm sorry that happened to you, but I am not going to let that happen to me, because I can see things before they happen."

"That's why I said don't jump to conclusions with Kevin, because you haven't seen that side of him that I have, and furthermore, about your little love of your life thing, you should be thanking him for what he has done to you."

"Why is that?" her mother said.

"Because look what it brought you: a great husband, a great provider, a great daddy, and a great cook. You should be jumping up and down on that. Plus, you were blessed with some beautiful children that are not so bad, and that love you with all our hearts."

"Awww," she said as she gave Pam a hug. "You are so sweet, and I do have a wonderful husband and a beautiful family, and you right, ya'll ain't so bad. Now, that brother of yours . . . now that's another story right there." They both started laughed and hugged each other as her mother held the baby in one arm.

"Okay, give me the pumpkin and you can go home to that beautiful family of yours," Pam started laughing.

"Child, please! Anyway," her mother said, "just do what you think is right for you and your baby, because you're right; I really don't know what's going on with Kevin."

"Oh, Mom, let me go get the mail right quick," Pam said as she handed the baby to her mother and went down the steps to the mailbox. She opened it, and there it was–the money wrapped around paper so that you couldn't tell what it is. She went back upstairs and got the baby from her mother. "Okay, Mama, I'll see you later."

"Okay, bye, baby," her mother said as she kissed Peter, then kissed Pam, and then went out the door. She turned back and said, "Oh, Kevin just called and said he made it home and call him when you get back."

"Okay, I will," Pam said. "Bye again." Pam put Peter in his baby swing and then called Kevin back. They had a good conversation, and Pam told him that her mom liked him for some odd reason.

"Why is that strange?" he asked.

"Because she really doesn't give guys a chance when it comes to me."

"Oh, really?" Kevin said. "Well, tell your mother that I will treat you like you need to be treated in life, and you do the same by me as well."

"What do you mean by that?" Pam asked in a curious way.

"Well, you know, I like to be pampered too at times."

"Oh, really now?" Pam said.

"Now, ain't nothing wrong with a woman showing love to her man who is making sure that his woman is taken care of. And in your case, your child as well."

"I hear you," Pam said, but she was starting to get a little mad, because she had never met a man like this, and pampering him was something she had never done, so she was very disturbed at the moment.

"Do you have a problem with doing for your man?" Kevin asked her.

"No, I don't. I just never had to, so this is a first for me. But, if I learn, I will definitely do it," Pam replied.

"Oh, okay, I just wanted to know, and that's no problem. I can break you out of that spoiled crap and make you into a full woman," Kevin said to her.

Pam was almost about to explode on him, but she kept her cool and said, "Oops, this is my job calling. I will call you back. Let me see what they want."

"Okay, that's fine," Kevin said as they hung up the phone.

"Freaking jerk! Ooh, he just send cramps all over me, he is so damn cocky." She grabbed Peter and said to him, "You all the man I need in my life." They went into the bedroom. She and Peter played, and she was teaching him how to talk and walk. She always had something for them to do, and she enjoyed every minute of it.

The next day at work, Pam got a call from Kevin around lunchtime and he asked if he could he take her out to lunch or take her and Peter to dinner. "Kevin, we need to talk," she said.

"About what?" Kevin said. "Is this about last night or something, because I see that might be a problem for you."

"It's not a problem at all, honey! It's your character," Pam said.

"My character? What's wrong with me having confidence in myself? Are you looking for a weak kind of man, or one who take care of business and take charge in his journey?"

"Neither one. I just want a guy who is loving and caring to me and my son, and I will be a caring person to whomever I am with, but your cocky attitude turns me all the way off at times."

"Look, baby girl, I'm just trying to understand, and what I need to do to have you and keep you," he said.

"Not with those sarcastic type remarks that you are making."

"I feel you on that, and I just ask you to work with me and help me control my mouth, because I have been told it is kind of foul at times," Kevin said, "so please forgive me. I don't mean any harm at all."

"Well, we will see," Pam said.

"I will see you at 5:00 p.m., okay?"

Pam stressed, "Okay, I hear you," she said as Kevin started to laugh. "Talk to you then," Pam said and they hung up the phone.

Kevin arrived on time, and Pam and Peter were ready. "So, this is the little man," said Kevin, as he tried to pick Peter up, but Peter started to cry like he had never done before in his little life.

"What's wrong, baby?" Pam took him from Kevin's arms. "It's okay, baby, everything is all right," she said as Kevin stood in shock.

"Wow! He is a little mama's boy, I see."

"No, he has never acted like this before with anybody," Pam said. "Maybe we should just call this off."

"No, no, no! I will just let him be with you and let him grow to like me, okay?" Kevin said as he opened the door for her and he put the car seat in and let her secure him into it.

They went to the restaurant, but Peter kept looking at Kevin's every move, like he knew what was going on with him. "Dang, he really is watching me like a hawk," Kevin said. "Man, he is already protective of his mama. Lil man, I will be good." Kevin raised his hands in the air like he was giving up. "You win. I will be on my best behavior with your mother; I promise, lil' man."

It was like Peter knew what he was talking about, because he gave him a look like, *You better leave my mama alone and get out of our lives.*

They ate, and Kevin took them home. When he dropped them off, he didn't help get the baby out or open the door for her, or help her take him upstairs. He had a call, and when he pulled up to her place, he didn't say *hold on* or anything; he just kept on talking. When she got into the house, she was so mad that she just shut her phone all the way off. She got Peter ready for bed, tucked him in, and told him, "Lil' man, God has given you a gift, and I saw it tonight. Mama is sorry about tonight. It won't happen again, I promise. She kissed him on his forehead. Peter started smiling, and then he went to sleep. Pam got in the bed and she went to sleep herself, thinking about when God was going to send the right guy for her.

Then she jumped up and said, "Why am I turning my phone off? I pay the bills around here." So, she turned on her phone, and right at the time she turned it on, it was ringing. It was Kevin.

"Hello?" she said.

"Man, I just got a ticket," Kevin said, as he was furious.

"How'd that happen?" Pam asked, smiling and smirking on the other end.

"I was coming out of the damn complex of yours and the police pulled me over, saying that I was speeding."

"Well, you need to calm down and stop yelling, because that's not going to make the problem go away," she said.

"Man, forget that! This would have never happened if I wouldn't have come over there and taken you and that little punk of a kid of yours out. I should have just stayed at home. Damn." Kevin was so pissed that he didn't even realize that Pam had already hung the phone up on him.

CHAPTER SEVEN

" GETTING MY OWN"

The next morning, Pam got ready for work, but instead of going, she called and told them that she wasn't going to make it in today because she needed to handle some business. Her job gave her the day off without any questions asked. Pam had been there for a long time, and she was very well liked at the job, so it was nothing for her to be off at any time. She called her mother and told her that she wasn't going to work, but she still wanted her to come by and get her at a later time to take her somewhere.

"Why? What's wrong with you?" her mother asked in a concerned voice. "After I drop your sister off I was heading that way. You know that this will break my normal routine."

"I know, Mama, but can you please just be here at 10:30? I will tell you when you get here, okay?"

"Lord, have mercy. What have you done now?" her mother said over the phone.

"Mother, it's nothing like you think it is. Trust me on that; I promise you," Pam said.

"Well, why can't you tell me, Pam? What's going on then?"

"Mom, just be here at 10:30." Pam was getting a little upset, and her mother knew it, so she said she would be at her house at 10:30.

They hung up the phone. Pam went in the living room so that she would not wake up the baby. She got on her knees and prayed on the couch. "Lord, I need you right now, Father, to show me where I need to be in my life. I have no luck with men and I'm tired of getting up early to catch the bus every day going to work when I could sleep at home longer if I had a car. God, please help me not fall by the wayside on making dumb mistakes in my life. Just please help me understand what I need to do in life. Father, I love you and honor you, in Jesus' name. Amen." She got up off her knees and just started praising God. See, she was ready to go to work, but something made her call in for some reason, and then she started thinking about how she had been getting $400 dollars a month ever since she was pregnant with Peter from someone she didn't know, but she had never spent the money. She always put it in the bank, so she just said, "Thank you, Jesus. Now I know what I need to do," and she turned on the TV and there was her confirmation. They had a first-time buyers' blowout sale and the sale ended today. "God, you are so awesome!" She screamed. "Oops! I forgot; my baby is asleep." She tiptoed to see if she had woken him up, but she hadn't.

She called the automated banking system to check her balance, and she was shocked that she had so much money in the bank that she could buy a car for cash. At this time, Pam just lay across the bed and chilled until her mother came to get her. As she was waiting, she dozed off for a minute, and she thought that she was dreaming when she felt somebody playing with her nose, but it got harder, and then it was like something wet was on her nose. She got up. It was Peter. "Boy!" She grabbed him and said, "How did you get out of your bed?" Pam had his bed against her bed, and pillows around the crib on the floor, so it looked like he got out and got up under his mother. "You are so amazing, but don't do that again, okay?"

As Peter looked at his mom and started laughing, she said, "It ain't funny. Don't do that. You might hurt yourself." Peter looked at his mother, then leaned forward and kissed his mama on the mouth and hugged her. She knew he was a special son that loved her so much. "Aww, thank you, Mama's baby," she said as she talked to him in her little high voice. At this time, her mother came and she told her that she wanted to buy a car and had saved up some money.

"How much money you got, honey?" her mother asked.

"I got enough to buy a car without a note," Pam said.

"Wow! How you do that? I need to go back to work." Her mother started laughing.

"No, Mama, I been getting that money still from the unknown person in the mail and I haven't spent any of it since I got it. I just been putting it in the bank. It's been 17 months, and they give me $400 a month, plus the $1,400 I put in there a month from my check and the money ya'll gave me for my graduation present. I think I got enough to buy one," Pam said as she gave her mother a high five.

"Well, go 'head then with your bad self, girl," her mother said.

"Well, with that said, let's ride." They had a great time out looking for a car, and got the best deal ever that they both said was nothing but God. She and her mother went to go get something to eat to celebrate her new car. Her mom asked how her date went with Kevin.

"Don't even ask about that clown," Pam said.

"Why? What happened?" her mom asked.

"Well, first off, Peter didn't like him. He didn't make sure we got in the house safe or even open the car door to help me get Peter out; he just stayed on the phone while I got everything out. Then, the ultimate was, he blamed us for him getting a ticket and said something negative about Peter, which is a big no, no."

"What?" her mother said.

"Yep. I told you he was a buster, but you felt something in your spirit," Pam said.

"Hell, that must have been heartburn, then, because I just thought he was a good guy."

"No, just a crazy jerk," Pam said.

"Well, it's good that you spotted that, lil' man," Pam's mother said to Peter while pinching his little fat cheeks.

"Yes, he is Mommy's little bodyguard."

"Keep them clowns from your mama, you hear, lil' man?" Peter started smiling.

"You see that, Mom? It is like he knows what you're talking about," Pam said to her mother.

"Don't nothing surprise me these days about kids, honey. They too much for me. I can tell you that much," her mother said as they got ready to go. They walked to Pam's new car and put the baby in. When they looked up, there was Kevin with another woman going into the restaurant.

Pam's mother hollered out his name. "Hello, Kevin!" He turned around and looked. When he saw them, Pam's mother waved and asked, "How are you today?"

He was so shocked and felt really stupid. He had a hard time saying anything. "I'm doing fine, and what about yourself?" he asked Pam's mother.

"Fine. Me, and my daughter, and my grandson just came out to dinner together to celebrate her new victory in life."

"Oh, okay." Then Kevin said, "Well, take care, and I'll talk to you later," and he went into the restaurant.

"Oooh, that just burns me up. Sorry, Mom," Pam said.

"Well, he should have just not done that crap, and was talking like he hadn't done anything wrong. That's what's burning me up."

"Mom, just calm down and get in your car and go home, okay? He is not worth it," Pam said, as she put her hands on her mom's shoulders. "It's all good. Trust me when I tell you that I'm just fine. I got me a new car and a new attitude," Pam said as they both started laughing about the whole situation. "Why should I go around with my head hanging down like I can't get no good man? Mama, watch how me and my baby pull out on them," Pam said as she put on her sunglasses, pulled off, and blew the horn at her mother as they went in the opposite direction.

Pam got home and she was so excited that she had bought a car. When she thought it couldn't get any better, she looked at her phone and couldn't believe who it was. "Hello?" she said.

"May I speak to Pam?" the voice on the other line said to her as she couldn't stop smiling. "This is she."

"Hey, how are you? Long time."

"Hey, stranger," she said in a pleasant voice. "Where have you been?" Pam asked.

"Well, first of all, do you know who you are talking to?" the other asked.

"Yes, I do. This is Peter."

"Yes, it is. Aaah, man, you remembered me, huh?"

"How could I forget you? What's been going on?" Pam asked, because she really had been missing Peter ever since he left and hadn't come back from his parents in the other country.

"I'm doing pretty well, I guess," he said.

"How are your parents doing?" Pam asked.

"They both are dead."

"What?" Pam said.

"Yep, I had to bury them both, so I'm just really trying to grasp it all right now."

"Baby, I am so sorry," Pam said as she started to cry, and then Peter started to cry as well.

"That's why I'm calling you, to see if anybody has come into your life, because I want to be a part of you and your baby's lives forever," Peter said to Pam.

"What, are you asking me to marry you?" Pam asked in a very serious tone.

"Yes, if you will have me in your life," he said.

"Yes! I will! Yes! Baby, yes!" she shouted.

"Well, I'm in town and I want to see you and they baby, if that's okay with you?"

"That's fine, baby. We are here waiting on you."

"Okay, I'm on my way."

"Okay!" Pam said as they hung up the phone.

Peter got there, and there were so many passionate feelings in the air and in the warmth that Peter brought to her heart. The feelings where so overbearing that they forgot about the baby until he made a noise. "Oh, I'm so sorry, baby," he said as she went to him, picked him up, and took him over to where Peter was standing. "Wow! He is so beautiful," Peter said. "Hey there, little man," he said as he reached for him, but the craziest thing was, little Peter was trying to get to Peter. Peter just hugged him and said, "You are my little prince." Then he asked Pam, "What's his name?"

"His name is Peter."

"For real?" Peter looked in shock, and said, "This is my little boy," he said as he kissed Peter's cheeks. "Wow! I'm so happy to see that you are doing well and everything," he said.

"Yes, I'm doing just fine, and I just bought a car today."

"For real? Which one is it?" he said.

"The black one."

He looked out the window and said, "That's yours? Wow! You really doing well. That's brand new right there," Peter said.

"Yes, it is, and I paid for it cash," Pam said.

"Baby, I'm so proud of you and what you have done in your life. I knew you was special," he said. "So, ya'll want to get something to eat?"

"No, we just ate with my mom."

"Oh, really? How is she doing?" he asked. "I mean, how is your whole family?"

"Everybody is fine. Everybody is still chilling."

"Okay, that's good. So, you think you family will approve of us getting married?" he asked.

"Baby, I don't care about what they think. I want to be happy, and I know I will be happy with you," Pam said. They kissed and held little Peter together in their arms like a perfect family.

Peter said, "Well, I have to fly out of town tonight, but I will be back first thing Friday. On Monday, I have a deal that I have to close in the morning, so I will be back and we will go from there, okay?"

"Baby, dang! You just got here," Pam said.

"I know, baby, but when I do this, we won't have to work anymore?"

"What do you mean *we*?" Pam said.

"Just like I said. We - me and you. This is ours. So, that's why I have to go and close this deal, okay baby?"

"Well, okay," Pam said in a very supportive voice.

Peter kissed Pam and little Peter on the forehead, and said to them, "Daddy will be back home Friday, and I love ya'll."

"We love you, too," Pam said, as little Peter started to cry.

Peter came back in, kissed him again, and told them he would be back as promised. Then he said, "I almost forgot," and reached in his pocket and gave her some money. "Here, take this for you and the baby," he said.

"No, we fine," Pam said, pulling her hand back.

"Well, just go shopping or something."

"No, I said, before you miss your plane," she said. Peter put it on the counter and went out the door. When he got to the airport, he called, and Pam was crying. He asked her what was wrong. She said she wished that Peter really was his son, and that she was sorry for what happened to her, and she wanted them to have a baby as well together.

"Baby, that wasn't your fault what happened to you," he said. "Don't you blame yourself for nothing that went on that day. I'm here, and I'm not going anywhere. That's my child, regardless of how he got here. That is my child, okay?"

"Okay," Pam said as she wiped her tears and told Peter that she loved him so much, and that he was a wonderful human being. She and little Peter would be waiting on his return, and she thanked him for the money he gave them.

"You are welcome. Is that enough?" he asked.

"Man, stop. Five thousand is more than enough."

"Because I love you," he said. "I don't have enough to give you for your love and compassion that you give me on a regular basis."

"You are so real and got yourself together."

"Well, let me get on this plane. I will call ya'll later."

"Bye," Pam said.

"Bye, bye," he said.

Pam was happy that Peter had come back into her life and she said that she was going to be the best wife she could be. Pam went to work the next day in her new car, and people let her know that it was nice and she did a good job picking it out. She told them thanks, but she really had her mind on Peter. It couldn't get to Friday fast enough for her. It seemed like the week was dragging, and she wanted it to speed up so that she could see Peter again.

As the days where getting closer, Peter would call every night and tell them goodnight, that everything was going well with the deal, and that they were very close to closing it. He would ask her to put the phone up to the baby's ear so that he could talk to him. Little Peter would just smile and try his hardest to talk back to him. Pam had made it all the way through Thursday. There was one more day to go before she saw her husband-to-be. At work, the day went by fast. She got in the car, and before she could pull off, she realized that she wanted it to be special when Peter got back, so she ran in the building and asked her boss if she could take another day off so that she could be there when he got in.

Her boss was like, "Girl, you must be in love, because I remember we had to force you to take your sick and holiday time. So yes, you can take off. We are fine here."

"Oh, thank you so much," Pam said, "and ya'll have a great weekend."

"And we hope you do the same," the people said in the office. "Don't do nothing we wouldn't do," they said.

"Oh, this time, I will," Pam said, and everybody started laughing as she got in her car and went straight to the mall. At the mall, she went to go buy something special for Peter's eyes only.

While in the mall, Peter called all excited. "We got it! We got it!" he said. "Baby, we set for life."

Pam started screaming, and everybody around her looked at her. "I'm so sorry everybody," she said.

"Who are you talking to, baby?" he asked.

"People in the mall. I screamed in the mall and everybody started looking at me, so I told them I was sorry."

"Oh, okay. I love you, and I will be touching down at 9:00 a.m. tomorrow."

"Well, I will be waiting for you, because I took the day off and I got a very little surprise for you as well," Pam said.

"Oh, really?" Peter said. "Boy, I can't wait to see it," he said.

"Well, I hope you don't look at it too long," Pam said in a sexy voice, like she was telling him that he would want to get to the surprise real fast. "I will be there, baby."

"Let me see if they've got an earlier flight coming in so I can get there quicker." They both laughed, and Peter told her that he loved her, and to kiss the baby for him. Pam was so excited that he was coming home that she went and bought some items just for her and her husband-to-be. She wanted tomorrow to be a very special day for the both of them.

Pam got home and just chilled out with the baby until he went to sleep in her arms. "Oh, I almost forgot to call my mama and see if she could come get the baby in the morning and watch him at their house so Peter and I can just have some private time alone." She called her mother and asked her if she could watch little Peter at her house because she has something to do tomorrow.

"What do you have to do?" her mother asked.

"I have to do something, Mama. Please just see if you can watch him over there tomorrow," Pam said in a whining voice.

"What are you up to, girl?" her mother asked. "Something doesn't sound right to me about anything."

"Well, if you must know, Peter came in town a couple of days ago and he asked me to marry him."

"What? Marry him?" her mother asked. "Lord, child, why can't you just wait instead of going from this one to that one?" her mother said.

"First of all, you act like I'm dating a lot of guys or something. Dang, I go out one time with a loser that you liked and now a person who has his life together is in my life and stepping up to the plate, not only for me, but for my baby as well. I can't beat that," Pam said.

"Well, does the baby like him?" the mother asked.

"No, he doesn't like him."

"Why not?" the mother asked. "See, you said yourself that Peter can pick out those who are up to something."

"I know, right? He can pick them right out. That's why Peter loves him and cried when he left. Peter had to turn around and calm him down before he left. Now what?"

"Well, lady, don't you be raising your voice at me and things," her mother said. "I guess since you happy, then I'm happy for you as well."

"Oh, really?" Pam said.

"Yes, really, honey. Now, don't push it. We ain't paying for nothing. Let his parents pay for the wedding since he got so much money," her mother said.

"He can't do that," Pam said.

"Why can't he do that? Just call them and they will be proud to do it," her mother said.

"Mom, they both died when he was out of the country," Pam said.

"Oh, I'm so sorry to hear that," her mother said. She wanted to just crawl up under a rock after Pam told her that. "Lord, have mercy. Jesus! I know that man is going through a lot of pain, and I'm sorry, Pam." Her mother started crying, because she felt lower than low about how she never gave the man a chance to just say hi or spend time with them without judging at times. "Wow, I just feel so stupid about everything I ever did to that man, and tell him he's got our blessings. We will pay for the wedding with no problems."

"Well, you should feel bad that you have talked about this man and on top of that, the deal that he closed today. He told me that we don't have to work anymore. Not just me, but him as well," Pam said. "Now you know you can't just find a person like that. We can both retire from the work world. That's why I want this to be special for him when he gets here."

"Okay, I can come get the baby tonight if you want me to," her mother said, since she was very sorry for saying what she'd said about Peter all this time.

"You will?" Pam said.

"Yes, I will," the mother said, "and I'm on my way now, so have him ready when I get there."

CHAPTER EIGHT

" THE SAGA CONTINUES"

Pam got the baby ready, and her mother came. Pam was so excited that she couldn't sleep at the time, and finally she woke up at 7:45. She jumped up and put her clothes on, and thought she was late for work, but after she got in her car, she realized that she didn't have her baby or have to go to work. "Lord! I need to get a grip on myself. I'm about to lose my mind," she said, as she walked back to her apartment. She went in the house and just set up everything that she was going to set up for Peter's special day back. As she was making everything perfect for him, she realized that she had forgotten a few things. She had to go to the store, and by the time she got home it was 9:15. She hadn't heard from Peter yet. She called his cell phone, but it was still off. She didn't panic; she just waited another 20 minutes, and then she panicked. "Man, I hope this man is not playing with my emotions, because I will be so through with him if he pulls some mess like that."

Pam just turned on the TV until Peter called. It was 10:00 a.m., and still no sign of Peter, so she called the airport to see if the plane had landed on time. She was furious with Peter, because she knew that he would call, but he hadn't and his phone was still off. So, she just sat and kept watching TV. Then, they came in with some breaking news that a plane had crashed on its way to the airport. It was coming in from another state, and they didn't think there were survivors from the crash. Pam was like, "See, God, let me stop thinking negative, because he could have been on that flight or something, but thank you, Jesus; he is in another state." Then, the news popped back in and said that the plane went up in flames, and that was when Pam's doorbell rang. She went to it, but it was only the mailman delivering the mail early that morning. She had a certified letter from someone.

She shut the door, and went back to watch the TV. They said that they had found the list of people on the plane, but that all were dead. They read off the list of people that were on the plane. As they read, Pam got up to grab an apple just as she heard something that sounded like Peter's name, but she knew that his flight landed at 9:00, and he just hadn't called yet. "See, I'm up here worried for this man, and he can't even realize that his phone is not on," Pam said as she tried again, but no answer. She just sat there looking at this plane crash. "Man, ain't no way somebody could have survived that plane crash," she said as she looked in sorrow. Just then, they posted the names on the TV. Pam grabbed some juice and started drinking it, when there it was: his name. She dropped the juice and her whole body went numb.

Peter hadn't caught the 9:00 flight because there was something wrong with it, so they had to put the passengers on two different planes, one at 9:00, and the other at 10:30. Peter couldn't call Pam because the signal couldn't be picked up in the airport, so he was going to call when he got there, but he never got the chance. Peter was dead. "Okay, that is not my baby! That is not my baby!" Pam screamed. "Okay, okay, okay! Let me calm down and just call the airport." She called and confirmed all the information, and it was him.

At this point, Pam was lifeless, with no care in the world. She couldn't hear, feel, or talk; nothing at this point. She just was in a state of shock. No one could break at that point. *Oh my God, what did you do? She looked up to the sky. How could you let this happen, Lord? How could you let this happen to me?* She fell to her knees screaming, "Lord, have mercy on me." It was the best day of her life, and all was taken from her in a matter of seconds.

Her mother called to just check on everything, but she didn't get an answer, and she didn't call back until that evening, but there was still no answer. She told her husband that she felt like something was wrong, and her husband was watching the news.

"This was an awful plane crash that happened this morning."

"What plane crash?" her mother said.

"They said it was a plane that burned up and there were no survivors."

"Oh wow! That is really sad," she said.

"I know their families are torn apart right now. I know that is something to just burn up like that," he said. "That is a hard way to go out in life, when you have to suffer through the pain and then fight for your life at the same time. I can only imagine how the people were feeling going through all of that."

"Yes, that is a way to go out, but you never know why God let that happen that way. However, it is a shame," Pam's mother said, and told her husband that she needed to run to the store to get the baby some more baby food, and could he watch him right quick and try to call Pam again, because she hadn't called or nothing. That wasn't like her.

"Ain't she with that guy?" her father asked.

"Yes, but still she would call and check in. I know Pam."

"Baby, she just probably having fun and when it's time to call, she will, and we can go over together and take the baby or keep the baby, since it is the weekend. Just let her have fun for a change."

"Well, you might be right," she said, as he took the baby and kissed her on the forehead.

She was walking toward the door, when she looked at the TV and thought she saw Peter's name. "Baby, I think I just saw Peter's name as one of those people on the plane."

"You sure?" he asked.

"I don't know, but I could have sworn that was that child's name. Maybe we should just check and see, please, because it just looked like his name, and plus, she isn't answering."

"Well, let's call one more time and see if she answers," he said. So they called, and this time, the mailbox was full. They got the baby and told the kids they were going over to their sister's house and would be right back. They got in the car and headed to Pam's house. When they got there, they saw her car, but something told her mother to just go check on everything. They got the baby, and opened the door. Before they could announce that they were in the house, they saw Pam sitting on the couch, her eyes were swollen shut. She was not even aware of who was in the house with her until her mother and father spoke to her. She had cried so much, her eyes had swollen so shut that she couldn't cry anymore.

"Oh, my, God. It was him on the plane," her mother said. "I am so sorry, baby." Her mother and dad hugged her while the baby was in his car seat on the couch next to his mother.

"Baby, I really don't know what to say to you. I mean, I just don't know." Her daddy started to cry. "I'm so sorry, pumpkin," he said, as he was holding onto her.

"He was going to marry me, Mama. He was going to take care of Peter and me for the rest of our lives. He was coming back to be a family. Now he is gone from us. I feel like I'm an old woman that's on her last leg. This is crazy," she said. "How can God allow me to go through all of this in my life at my age? How? I just don't understand none of this. He let me get raped. He let me lose the one person that really loved me for me. All I can do is ask, why me?"

She lay with her head in her daddy's chest, trying to understand the one that was bigger than everybody: God. She was really feeling right now like she had been following the wrong person or spirit all this time. She thought that the Devil was doing all of this to her, and even worse than that, she was thinking God didn't really exist, because there was no way on God's green earth that he would let something like this happen to anyone that followed him all the way in life. That was just impossible to think of.

A couple of days went by, and the people from the apartment complex came to see Pam, doing everything they could to comfort her, because they knew that Peter really loved Pam. While they were over her house, another certified notice came. She said, "Let me just go see what it is, and I do need to get some air." She went to the post office, and when she got out of the car, she freaked out because she thought that she had left her baby, but then realized that her parents had the baby with them a couple of days ago when everything happened.

"Wow! Please pull yourself together," Pam said to herself as she walked toward the entrance of the post office. She went in and picked up the package. It was a letter from Peter. She ran to the car, and just sat in it and said, "Why would he write me this letter instead of talking to me?" she said. "But how do I know it's a letter? Lord, I really don't know what it is, and I'm scared to open it and see."

She pulled off and went over her parents' house to let them read it. She went over and put the letter on the table, and told them that it was from Peter as she paced back and forth across the kitchen floor rubbing her arms like she was cold. "Calm down," her father said. "Everything will be all right." He grabbed her gently and sat her down in a chair.

Her mother asked whether she wanted her to read it. "I don't care who reads it, but I'm not." Everybody was standing in the kitchen waiting to hear what Peter wrote or sent to Pam. As her mother reached for the letter, Pam started shaking harder.

"Girl, you got to calm down. You making us nervous with all that now," her mother said. Her mother grabbed the letter and read it. It said, "*Hey, I know you thinking like why in the world is he writing me instead of talking to me? LOL.*—What does LOL mean?" Pam's mother asked.

"Laugh out loud," everybody said at the same time.

"Well, excuse me," her mother said. "Anyway, it says: *LOL, but my heart hasn't stopped hurting for my parents since they died and left me all alone in the world. But since you let me in your life again, I didn't want to miss an opportunity of losing out again on something I love so dearly. I hope your parents will try to understand me and give me a chance to prove myself to them, but I'm really not worried about them, because I let God fight my battles. I don't have nothing to prove to them. I'm from the same person that made them, and I have hang-ups just like they have hang-ups. They can't judge me without getting judged themselves by a higher power than I will ever be. When I saw that little prince, I felt like he was my son, and there was no way he was going to grow up without a father in his life. That's why, when I get back in town, I want to adopt him and make him mine. If that's okay by you. I really wrote you because a feeling came over me that I can't describe, but it was a feeling of peace now in my life. No more worries; no sorrow; no more sadness. It felt different, so I just got down on my knees and started to pray and ask God to forgive me for all my sins and unrighteous acts that I have done, and accepted Jesus Christ as my lord and savior again. I told him I loved him, and would honor him for the rest of my life. I know he sent you into my life, and no matter what happens to me, please let someone love you and take care of you when the chance comes.*

"Baby, I don't know why I'm saying this when I'm the one it's going to be, but I just had something come across me to write to you. I will never try to stop you from being happy. That's why I took out an insurance policy. I went back to the office and got all of your information, and if anything happens to me, you will be taken care of. I know nothing is going to happen to me, and I tried to get the little man's social security number, but I couldn't find it. I just doubled the policy that went into effect yesterday, so it is good now. Don't be

trying to kill me, or anything like that, like having me go get the mail or something and somebody drives up on me. LOL. Anyway, it is for two million dollars, one for you and the other for Peter, Jr. I hope you don't mind me calling him that. Anyway, I will see you and make you read this in my face, so when you get to this part of the letter, I will be on one knee, asking for you hand in marriage. See!!!? Look down!!! Bam!! See, you soon. I will always love you. He signed it: Peter, your knight in shining armor."

"Wow!" her father said.

"Hell, I want to marry him my damn self," the mother said. "Oops! I mean, baby. You know what I mean."

Pam had a smile on her face and said, "I won't let him down as he was a great person. I will stay focused and make the best of my child's life and mine."

Days went by and they had a small but very nice funeral. Everybody knew Pam and who she was without her knowing anybody. "Hi, I am Peter's cousin, Shawn. Nice to finally meet you, Pam."

"Nice to meet you, too, Shawn. Peter used to talk about you all the time, and I'm just glad you came, even though it's not the best time." They gave each other hugs, and Pam talked to all his people, She also got their numbers and said that they would keep in touch with each other.

Pam's life had to continue, so the money she got each month was still coming, and she had two million that had made interest since Peter's death.

CHAPTER NINE

" A CHANGE OF SCENERY"

It had been five years since his tragic death, and lil' Peter was in school, and playing little league football and basketball. Pam really kept him involved in things to keep that man in him, since it was just her without a man around. Pam was enjoying life, but it was hard on her sometimes, not with money, but with being without that companion in her life.

One day, Pam was coming home from work when her car started jerking and shaking, but she made it home. She called her dad and he had somebody look at it for her. They came out and supposedly fixed her car for her. It ran for the rest of the week, and when the weekend hit, it still was doing fine, until she stopped at this restaurant with Peter and got something to eat. When they finished, the car did the same thing, but this time, it was gone. It had run its last race.

"Aww, man," Peter said. "I was trying to get home and watch the game."

Pam tried to call her dad, but no answer, nor was there an answer with her mom. So, she called AAA to come tow her car.

A car pulled up in front of her, and this guy got out and came toward the car. Pam was looking kind of scared, but in her mind, she was like, *Wow, he looks great.* He approached the car and asked if they needed help.

"Huh?" Pam said as she kept the window rolled up, so she really couldn't hear him.

"I said, do ya'll need any help?" the guy screamed.

"Oh, I'm sorry. I still got the window up," Pam said.

"No problem. I was asking if ya'll need any help?"

"Well, my car won't start and I was just calling a tow truck to tow it for me. I just got it worked on a couple of days ago," she said.

"Well, what is it doing?" he asked.

"Nothing," Pam said, but it was just jerking and then it just cut off.

"You mind if I take a look at it?"

"Sure, knock yourself out," Pam said. The guy looked, and in about 40 seconds, he told her to try cranking it. She tried, and it came on. "Thank you so much."

"No problem. Glad to be of help," he said.

"Wow! I was just about to call to have it towed."

"No, you just need to get a filter from the parts shop, because I took the old one out, but you can ride for a couple of days on it," he said.

"Filter? I don't know anything about a filter," she said. He started laughing and told her that she could go up to the one up the street and he would put it in for her. She said that was fine, they went and got the part, and he put it in. "Thanks again."

"Terry," he said as he put his hand out.

"Huh?"

"My name is Terry Vinson."

"Okay, well, Terry, thanks. My name is Pam, and this is my son, Peter."

"Hi Peter. Nice to meet you. It looks like you play football or something."

"Yes, I play," Peter said.

"What position?"

"I play running back and linebacker."

"Oh, okay, you bring the pain on both ends." They both started laughing. "Well, let me let ya'll get on with ya'll's day. I was just out; I just stay down the street in the gated apartments."

"What apartments?" Pam asked. Terry told her the name. "Those are the ones we stay in."

"For real?" Terry said.

"Yes," she said.

"Wow, what a small world. Well, it was good to help a neighbor out, and I would love to see little big man play a game one day, but I wouldn't want anybody to get mad or anything like that," he said.

"If you are thinking that I'm married or dating anyone, I'm not, so you can come."

"Well, that is just great. I will be at the next one," he said. "You just let me know when and where I need to come, and I will be there."

Pam told him when Peter's next game was as they both went in, but Terry stayed in the next building.

So, they met up at the game and Terry was all in it. Pam said, "Dang. You have any children or something in sports?"

"No, I wish I had a child. I love little boys and I just love them even more when they love sports," he said. Terry told him Peter had a great game, and that he was proud of him. "So, can I treat ya'll to a victory lunch?" he asked.

Peter said, "Can we, Mom? I'm a little hungry."

"Well, I don't see why not. Sure, we would love to."

"Well, since the park doesn't stop playing until the night, maybe you can just leave your car here and we could go in mine, that's if you don't mind," Terry said.

"No, we can do that."

They went out to eat. They talked, and he brought them back to their car. Terry, once again, told them that he enjoyed spending time with them, and thanked them. "Hopefully, we can do this again sometime," he said. Pam looked, and asked him if he had a problem calling her sometime so that they could talk about the schedule instead of her bumping into him. She just did that to give him her number. They went their separate ways.

"Hey, Mom, I really like Terry. He is really cool and he knows stuff, and he said that he would teach me new stuff," Peter said.

"Yeah, he seems to be cool, and I like him, too," Pam said with a little grin on her face. All through football season, they went together to the games, and Terry would pick them up and take Peter to and from practice if Pam didn't have time. Terry worked from home, so he really had time to do things. If he had to keep working, he would have his computer with him, and sit and watch and do his work. Terry was also tops at his company, and he was just a few years older than Pam. Pam's family loved him as well, and they seemed to be happy around each other, going to the mall, horseback riding, just doing everything together. Basketball season, baseball, school events, you name it; Terry was there for almost everything if he could be there.

Time had gone by that nobody realized, and this had been going on for five years. Terry and Pam were so close, but she was taken aback when Terry asked to marry her. She choked up, and Terry asked her what was wrong, so she told him, and he said, "I'm not trying to sound shallow, but he is dead and gone, and I'm sure he would want you to be happy in life."

"Yes, he said that in a letter he wrote me. It was like he knew he was going to die or something."

"Well, they say you know when you are going to die," Terry said, "but all I know is that I love you both, and I don't want anybody else in my life but you and Peter."

"Yes, and Peter just loves you, too. Hell, ya'll even starting to look like each other since ya'll been around each other so much. People be asking him if you are his daddy."

"Well, I want to be, and your husband, your provider, your best friend, everything to you, if you just say yes," he said.

Pam said, "Yes, I will marry you," and they kissed. Then, Pam said, "But before we get married, don't fly on any planes or anything like that, okay?"

"Okay, baby," Terry said as they embraced some more.

Later that day, they went by his parents' home and told them. They were happy. Next, they went by her parents' house and told them, and Pam was surprised at her mother for saying, "About time." Pam just knew her mother was going to flip, but she didn't, so Terry and

Pam became a couple, and Terry and Peter got very close. Terry would help him with his homework and talk to him about guy stuff.

Terry was getting Peter ready for high school. He was so good in sports that different high schools wanted him, but since they moved away from everything, Peter had to be taken to school, because nothing came that far out. They stayed in a state-of-the-art house. Terry was a computer and electronic junkie. That was what he did for a living, and that way, Pam didn't have to work anymore. The house was 12,000 square feet, with everything in it that you could imagine.

When Pam moved, the money stopped coming for Peter. In all these years, 13 to be exact, she received $400 each month, without ever knowing who it was from. She told her husband, and he said, "Maybe he found out you were married and knew he couldn't get you anymore." They both started laughing.

Peter had a great first year at all the sports, but his passion was clearly football and basketball. So, by this time, it was his freshman year in high school, and it was like he grew overnight or something. "Wow! Baby you're not that little kid anymore, huh?" Pam said as her mother now looked up at him. "You are now one of the big boys." Pam started laughing and patted him on his back.

"Yeah, son, you did just grow overnight," Terry said. Peter became one of the best backs in the nation, and he was only a freshman. His grades were so good, that he was already taking college courses in high school. He was before his time. No one could touch him in sports, and he told his mother that he would make sure she would never want for nothing in life if he made it.

With the fame came things like girls, and Peter could have anybody he wanted, whether a freshman or a senior. He was loved by everybody, but he only wanted this one particular girl, and her name was Kayla. She was cute, smart, and she really didn't pay Peter any attention. That turned him on even more. She would go to class and see him in the hall, but she would just wave and keep going. Peter wanted her real bad, so he went up to her one day and asked, "Why don't you ever speak to me?"

"Hi, my name is Kayla," she said as she put her hand out to shake his. He stood there looking confused.

"What did you do that for?" He shook her hand.

"Because, I'm not one of your fan people, so when you go up to anyone, you don't start by saying, 'why don't you ever speak?'" she said. "I'm just showing you the proper way of doing it."

"Okay, I can understand that," he said to her. "Can we start over with this introduction?"

"Well, we will try later, but right now, I need to get to class. You know, some people come to school to learn, not to meet people." She shut her locker and walked away.

"Wow! I love that girl."

He went to class himself, but the weird part was they didn't see each other a lot, although they both were smart. After school he would see her, but he had to go to practice, so they would just speak and keep going. A couple of days went by, and this time, Terry approached Kayla the correct way. From that day on, they were a couple.

Peter cut off all the extra madness around him with no problem, and really focused on his relationship with Kayla. She was at every game, and they would meet up at the library sometimes and do homework together, but they had been together for six months, and neither one of their parents knew about their relationship. "Baby, do you think we need to go on and tell our parents that we are seeing each other?" Kayla said.

"Well, I really don't know, because I don't want anything negative said about us," Peter said in a concerned and mean voice.

"Baby, calm down and just listen. Our grades have not fallen off, and we haven't been doing anything really out of the ordinary. You and I respect each other and I think that we are good together. What do you think?" Kayla said as she put her arms around Peter's neck and looked him in the eyes with passion and love.

"I will talk to my parents tonight," he said.

"Me too," and they kissed, and hugged, and went home.

CHAPTER TEN

" IT'S ALL COMING TOGETHER"

Later that night, when Pam and Terry were in the living room watching TV, Peter walked in and asked if he could speak to them about something. "Sure baby, what's up?" Pam said.

"Well, it's like . . ." Peter began to stutter. "It's like . . . I'm in– I mean, I have a girlfriend, and her name is Kayla, and we been together for six months now, and I love her."

"What!? Man, slow down! You talking too fast," Terry said. "Now, slow down and tell us what you are talking about."

Peter got himself together and told them that he had a girlfriend and her name was Kayla. He said he was in the same grade he was in, and took college courses as well, that she was very supportive in his life, and she was just everything he wanted in a girl. "So, she is not a distraction?" Pam asked.

"No, Mama, we been going to the library together, and, as you can see, my grades haven't fallen. We have just not said anything because we wanted to make sure that we were comfortable with each other first before we told ya'll."

"How comfortable did ya'll get?" Terry asked.

"Not like that." Peter kind of got upset about that remark.

"Hey! All right, now! Pump you brakes!" Terry said. "I just want to know so that you don't get caught up in life, that's all. I'm concerned about you and your well-being in life."

"I understand that, and I will not let ya'll down. I promise everything will stay the same with me."

"Well, I don't have a problem with it, do you, babe?" Pam asked.

"Oh no, not at all," Terry said. "I'm proud of you, and I'm glad you are talking about a girl, not nothing else. Whew!" and they all started laughing.

"So, when do we get to meet this Kayla person?" Pam said.

"Well, she's supposed to be talking to her parents as well, so we will see. I hope they cool with it like ya'll are."

"Well, we just trust you and hope you use better judgment in your life at times when it is needed, and not to be so quick to jump into things. The way you talk, you took time and really looked at everything about this person, and we know you young, but you are good so far with that," Terry said.

Over on Kayla's end, it was a little different; not in a bad way, but come to find out her daddy was a fan of Peter's, and she didn't know it. So, he wished she had told them sooner. So everything worked out, and all the parents met, and even started having get-together at each other's homes. Terry and Kayla dated all through high school, and when they were seniors, they both got full scholarships and were going to the same college. They had gotten so high in their work that they both made headlines for graduating early from high school and going to college, but they both wanted to go to the prom of their senior year. They went to their senior prom and had a great time, but something was missing, and they knew this was the biggest step in both of their lives. Even though they had already been accused of it, they'd never done it, and tonight they wanted it to happen, so this would be a day they wouldn't forget.

They had gotten a room earlier that week reserved in a private hotel that really no one their age would know about. They went into the room, and Kayla went into the restroom to freshen up a little. Peter turned on the TV and watched a movie that was already on. When Kayla came out, all of his attention went to her. "Wow! You look fabulous," he said.

"You like?" she said.

"Hell yes! That right there is wow." Kayla had put the outfit in her little purse that looked like nothing could fit in it, so you can imagine what the outfit looked like. Peter had never seen Kayla's body, only in biker shorts, but he'd never seen her flesh. He got up and kissed her gently, and after that, they made it the best night that they would never forget in their whole lives.

The next day, Peter called, to check on Kayla and see how she was feeling about the previous night. When he called, she answered the phone and said she was still tired from last night; so a little smile came over Peter's face when he heard that. He told her that he was going to cut the grass, so if he didn't answer the phone, then that was why. They hung up. Peter was so full of life that his parents asked him what was wrong with him. "Nothing; just happy this morning, that's all," he said. Terry knew what that was about, but didn't say anything, however he had a little grin on his face.

When they got through with breakfast, Peter said that he was going to cut the grass. "Now I know something is wrong with you," Pam said. "You are going to cut the grass when we usually have to beg and threaten you to cut it? Now you want to?"

"Baby, leave the man alone. If he wants to cut the grass, then let him cut the grass," Terry said.

"Yeah, you go ahead and cut that grass, and Terry, you go help him cut it," she said.

"Why I got to help him cut? He knows how to cut," Terry said.

"Yeah, Ma, why does he have to help me? I can do it by myself," Peter said.

"Yeah, we know that, but he need to teach you how to cover up the tools if it starts raining. If you let the rain hit that grass, then you could have more than you wanted out there to cut." Both Terry and Peter looked at each other like they had no idea what she talking about. "Play stupid if ya'll want to. Don't be bringing no kids around here, Peter. Now, you did what you did last night. I hope you used protection with that girl."

"Mom, what are you talking about?" Peter said with a little smirk on his face, and Terry just burst out laughing, because Pam knew why Peter was so happy and eager to do things.

"I wasn't born yesterday. You see when your daddy gets up painting, washing clothes, cleaning toilets . . . Yeah, he does the same thing. So, go pull that crap with somebody else besides me. I didn't make it this far by being stupid by no means," Pam said as she cleaned up the kitchen.

"Yeah, I think I will go out there and help my son a little in the yard," Terry said.

"Yeah you do that," Pam said.

"Let's go, son, before she really go off!" She shook her head while she finished cleaning up. "Well, son, you took a big step with that last night, and as long as you used protection . . . I didn't want it to happen, but hell, you probably have done it even before last night," Terry said.

"No, that was the first time last night," Peter said.

"Well, son, just cut the grass and have your moment." He patted his son on the back and told him that he was very proud of him, and that he was everything he'd always wanted in a son, and thanked him for allowing him to enter into his life. They hugged and told one another that they loved each other.

Peter was cutting the grass and was thinking about how Terry came into his and his mother's lives at the right time. Was that car meant to break down, or did God see fit for his mother and him to be happy with this man? He was confused and wanted to just talk to his mom about his real daddy, what happened to him, and why he never came around in his life. After Peter got done with the grass, he took a shower and got dressed. Kayla called and asked him if he missed her.

"Yes! I do," he said.

"How much?"

"A whole lot," Peter said as he was scratching his head thinking if these were trick questions or something.

"Well, if you saw me, would you kiss me and hold me tight?" she asked.

"Yes, I would," he said as he turned around, and she was right behind him.

"Well, do it," Kayla said.

"Wow, how did you get in?" he asked.

"Look, don't worry about that. Just do what you said you was going to do to me." They started kissing, and Peter just held her tight in his arms. They let each other go, and Kayla said that while he was in the shower, she came over and his parents let her in. "They told me that you was in the back, and they let me back here, which was strange."

"I know, right? They never done that before, but I think they did it because they know what we done last night."

"What? You told them?" Kayla asked in an embarrassed voice.

"No, they just figured it out. I don't know."

"I'm like so embarrassed about that," Kayla said. "They probably think I'm a whore now or something."

"No, baby, they cool with us," he said as he kissed her on the forehead. They both watched a couple of movies, and then Kayla went home.

As she walked out of the house, she gave both of his parents hugs, and both of them said, "Bye, Kayla."

She turned fire red, she was so embarrassed. She said goodbye, and was covering her face at the same time. Terry said, "Well, I got to go fix this woman's computer right quick and I'll be right back."

He left, and Peter thought that this was the perfect time for him to talk to his mother. "Mom, is it all right for us to talk?"

"Sure, honey, what's on your mind?" she asked.

"Well, it's about my dad," he said.

"What about him?" Pam asked.

"Well, I just wanted to know a little about him. You know what his name was; what he looked like; why he never came around us."

"Well, Peter, to be honest with you, I don't know who he is," Pam said.

"What do you mean you don't know who he is? You don't know who you were sleeping with at the time?"

"To be quite honest, no, I don't."

"How is that?"

"I was raped, okay? Since you must know, God told me to keep you, and here you are."

"Mama, I'm so sorry for taking you back to that moment of your life." They both started to cry.

"I'm sorry, Peter," she said. "I'm so sorry."

"Sorry for what?" he said. "You are the best person I will ever know, and I thank you, and I'm sorry for bringing back this mess," he said.

"Baby, I always wanted the best for you, and we were doing just fine with or without a man, but God, the ultimate man, brought Terry into our lives to make us complete. I'm so thankful for him, and I hope that even though he isn't your real father, he has been there like one," she said.

"I can't agree with you more," Peter said. "When I see him, I want to be like him and like you, and when I'm with Kayla, she reminds me a lot of you, so independent, and a family person. She loves to uplift people in their times of need," he said.

"Well, she is a wonderful girl. I love her a lot, and I hope ya'll don't get distracted by the outside world. It can really mess you up in a lot of ways," his mother said as they finished the conversation about who Peter's father was. They just chilled together and played like they used to do when Peter was young. Time sure had gone by so fast that now he was going to college, and on top of that, on a full scholarship. "Ain't God awesome?"

"Yes, he is," Peter said.

They all enjoyed the rest of the night as a family when Terry got back home. The time came and went by for the summer. It was time for Peter to go off to college, and he was excited as well as his dad was, but Pam didn't like it too much. Everybody came over to give a going-away party for him and Kayla. Her parents, Terry's parents and close people they knew in their lives were all there. Pam was thinking that in two days, her son would be going off to college. It was something that she didn't want to do, but Peter wanted it. She was so proud of him, and he was proud of her and what she had gone through in her life. The party went well, and Peter and Kayla took a walk around the yard. They were talking about old times, how they met, and the things they did together. Now, they were going to college together. "Whoever would have thought that?" they said.

"You never know how God got things worked out for you. Just be prepared, and go with the flow," Peter said.

Peter already had a jump on Kayla at college because he was so good that he was at practice with the college before he even lived on campus. When they got there on the first day, Peter told her that he wanted to surprise her and his parents and her parents. "What is it?" she said.

"Well, ya'll know I've been practicing with the team, right?"

"Yeah," everybody said.

"Well, I made the team, and I'm the starting running back for them."

"That's my boy," his daddy said.

"That's my son-in-law," Kayla's daddy said. They danced around like they had just hit the lottery.

For him to be on a top-ranking team and starting was a biggie for anybody. He was starting for the Texas Longhorns and on the first play of the first game, Peter ran a 98-yard touchdown. He was the leader, and he set all kinds of records in one game. Peter kept this going on for three years before the NFL wanted him ASAP. His mother supported his decision to leave early, while Kayla stayed in school because she wanted to be a doctor. Everybody was happy, but on draft day, he was chosen by a team that was nowhere near the family. However, when the team found out how good he was, they had no problem making sure that both of his parents could come, as well as Kayla. They would be flown in by a private jet. Everything worked out fine for them.

Eventually, Peter and Kayla got married and had a couple of kids themselves. They were having a great time in life.

Terry started to develop a cough that came off and on, but one particular day, it couldn't stop. They gave him cold medicine, but it didn't work. At his annual check-up, they couldn't see anything, but they gave him some strong antibiotics this time, trying to kill off whatever it was. For a few days, he was doing fine. He watched, as Peter was setting records in his 10th year in pro football. His son was a household name in homes around the world. Terry was proud of his son's success, and his little boy was growing up the same way, because he loved sports as well. When Terry had time, he would go see his son play.

It was just a sight to see, but one day, Terry couldn't make it to a game. He had this bad cough, and it had stopped, but this time, it came back worse than ever. They rushed him to the hospital, and this time, they did an MRI and found that he had cancer all through his body from his throat to his stomach, and it was spreading up to his brain. They rushed Terry into surgery, trying to find out how to stop it from doing any more damage to him, but it had gotten so bad that it was impossible to stop. The doctors told them the news, but he was recovering, and they were going to try and give him chemotherapy and see if that worked.

The next couple of days, Terry was too weak to talk, and finally it was like a miracle with him; he just got a burst of energy from out of nowhere. He asked to see everybody, and they let everybody come in his room. He told them he loved them and that he was sorry about what happened. They all told him it was not his fault. "We are just thanking God right now for you."

He said, "Thank you," but he wanted to talk to Pam alone. Everybody went out of the room, and he told the nurses not to come in while he was talking to Pam. They granted him that time. "Pam, I have something to tell you, and I want you to listen good, okay?"

"I'm listening," she said.

"You know I love you and Peter, and everybody else, but I really love you and Peter the most," he said.

"Okay, we know this," Pam said.

"Pam, I done something real bad in my life, and this is God's punishment to me," he said.

"Stop talking crazy now. Just get some rest."

"No, no, no; listen to me. I'm the one that raped you that night when you came home from work," he said.

In shock, Pam said, "Stop talking crazy."

"No, Pam, it is true. I raped you."

"Well, how did you do it?"

"One day, you was in the little convenience store and you dropped your credit card. I picked it up and gave it to you. I followed you home. You were walking and I found out where you stayed. Once I did, I moved into the apartments myself, but at this time, I saw the owner with you and I asked the people at the front desk if ya'll was dating. They just said they really didn't know. So one night, I saw a guy storm out of your apartment, and the next day I saw you alone. I followed you to your door in all black. I didn't want to hurt you or anything, but I just did something that I wish I wouldn't have done. After, I saw that you were pregnant. I started sending you $400 a month until we got married. Even when we were dating, I kept sending it to you. That's why Peter looks like me. It is not because he has been around me, but because I am his father."

Pam couldn't believe what she had just heard. "I can't and don't believe you," she said.

"It's true. I want you to have Peter draw blood and take mine, and see if I'm lying. I asked God for forgiveness right after it happened, but now I'm asking you," he said to Pam.

"After all this time, you want me to forgive you? How dare you?" She went out the room.

She didn't know how to tell Peter, but she did, and he agreed on the blood work. They ran the test, and it came back 99.9%. Terry was Peter's father. Terry had been let back in this child's life to raise him and watch him grow into a fine man. Peter and his mother came in the room together. "Man, how could you do something like that? Who gave you the right to do something like that?" Peter said.

"Son, I don't know, but I'm sorry," Terry said. "Will you forgive me?" he asked Peter.

"Yes, I will, because you did taught me how to become a man."

Pam said, "If my son can forgive you, I can, too."

"Thank ya'll so much," Terry said. They started crying and hugging each other. "That's all God wanted to hear from ya'll is that ya'll forgave me for my sin like he did. I never meant to cause ya'll any sorrow or pain in each one of ya'll lives." He kissed his boy and told him that he loved him.

"I love you, too, Daddy."

Then, he kissed Pam and told her the same thing, and she said she loved him as well. "Can I have one more of them family hugs? It felt so good to me," Terry said.

"Sure you can," Pam said as they hugged again. Everybody took a deep breath and let out a sigh of relief, but Terry, the father, the provider—the rapist—took his last breath for good. He had cleaned his slate with God, so he called him on home with a smile. All Pam and Peter could do was stand there and watch God do his work. Peter went on to be one of the greatest football players ever, and Pam lived to see her grandchildren have kids. An awesome life for one of God's true soldiers.

At the end of the day, no matter what you do or say, your goals, dreams, and journey in life always will be filled with trials and tribulations. But through it all, whether good or bad, you will reap what YOU HAVE SOWN...

ABOUT THE AUTHOR:

Dion Williams is a native of Atlanta, Georgia. He is a former sports recruiter for The National Football League who has represented some of the top football players in the league. He also worked as a football coach and personal trainer throughout his life, both in Pop Warner, and Arena league. After several years of weathering his own storms, he decided to take his life in a different path. His travels down some rough roads inspired him to reach, harder to do God's work. Today, Mr. Williams is known within his community as a minister, pastor, and friend with the soul to help others. *Through the Storm* is his first novel, and is a work of fiction. Through Pam's harrowing journey, he hopes you will find that everything around you may not really be what it seems to be. He reminds you that through your own storms in life, you can always find a little light to shine on you to help you reach the end of your journey.